"I always notice a lady's ankles," he replied unceremoniously. "Even a young lady's. I thought yours showed definite promise."

Grace straightened her shoulders, lifted her chin and said in her new childish voice, "Don't you think it's time to leave, Papa?"

"Yes, Doll." When he shook his head from side to side and laughed, he looked ten years younger and much more attractive. "What's the matter?" he demanded, seeing her studious gaze.

"You were to call me Augusta, because of its being Grandma's name," she reminded him.

"I'll try to remember," he said.

As Grace left the room with Whewett behind her, she had an instinctive feel he was looking at her ankles. They almost tingled with imagined perusal. . . .

MADCAP MISS

Joan Smith

FAWCETT CREST • NEW YORK

A Fawcett Crest Book
Published by Ballantine Books
Copyright © 1989 by Joan Smith

Library of Congress Catalog Card Number: 89-91421

ISBN 0-449-21695-0

Manufactured in the United States of America

First Edition: January 1990

Chapter One

Grace Farnsworth ripped the blue feather from her bonnet, tossed it into a dustbin, then retrieved it and stuck it into her pocket. She set the bonnet on her head, rolled back the brim, and surveyed herself in the mirror. Satisfied, she put her fingers inside the band of her blue serge suit skirt, hiked it up eight inches, and rolled it under several times, pulling her jacket down to conceal the resulting lump. This done, she examined herself in the mirror and smiled at the results. For the first time in her life she was thankful for her petite body. She did not look a day over thirteen and meant to pass for twelve on the coach, in order to pay the lower children's fare.

Grace was neither a nip cheese nor a thief, in the normal way. In her reticule there rested sufficient funds to get a child to Wickfield, with two shillings left over. She had paid full fare from Pevensey to Lewes and would gladly have done the same to

Wickfield had she had the money. It was imperative for her to get to Wickfield. She had just been summarily relieved of her post as governess to Mrs. Bixworth's two girls, due to Ellie Lou's running into the sea while romping on the beach. Naturally the governess was held at fault. She should have been watching Ellie Lou while simultaneously riding herd on Dora, who was intent on making mischief with an unleashed dog.

Really she was well out of the Bixworth residence, badly as she needed the job. If she had not half wanted to be let go, she would not have flared up at her mistress, telling her that what her daughters needed was not a governess but a sound thrashing.

She had very nearly got one herself, till she threatened to have the constable down on the harridan's head. Vulgar, bad-tempered shrew! She would never have to see her red face again—and never get the three weeks' wages that were owing to her, either. No matter. Miss Thomas would put her up till she found a new position. She was a greenhorn to have taken the first thing that was offered, but she had already billeted herself on her ex-governess for a month. Miss Thomas was in straitened circumstances, and Grace, though she was only five feet and one inch tall, ate like an infantryman.

Miss Farnsworth felt badly about battening herself on Miss Thomas. She had assumed that when her father died, she would come into a comfortable competence. She thought she might have to give up her home, but that she would be obliged to work for her keep never once occurred to her. Fortunately her ex-governess and later companion had saved up a nest egg. Miss Thomas had hired a cottage at Wickfield, where she had been born and reared. It was unconscionable to inflict herself on poor Thomas again. She would repay every penny.

Miss Farnworth's firm chin jutted out, giving her the air of a stubborn child as she stood looking at the brown-haired, brown-eyed girl in the mirror. After rendering thanks to God for her small body, she added a word on the subject of freckles, highly visible now with the rice powder washed away. She never thought she would be happy for them, the bane of her existence at a time when she had no real problems.

She picked up her straw case and walked out the door, causing no heads to turn as she left the inn. It was a busy place, where a child could pass unnoticed. In five minutes the stage ought to be leaving. The ticket agent's only question when she asked in a high voice for a child's fare was, "Are you traveling alone, missie?"

"Yes, sir, but only to Wickfield to meet my governess," she answered, smiling sweetly.

The stage was ready to leave. The only passenger, a stout matron of middle years, eyed Grace curiously, but soon glanced out the window to view a more interesting sight. A tall, dark-haired gentleman with an angry hue to his face was dashing toward the carriage, waving his hand. "Hold it!" he shouted. "Is there a spare seat?"

"Aye, mate, you're in luck," the driver called.

The newcomer fished in his pocket, handed up his money, as he had no ticket, and opened the door to enter. The two women looked with interest to see a gentleman of the first stare taking the common stage. As the carriage lurched forward, he grabbed

3

the window ledge. Both women noticed his elegant tanned-leather gloves. "What a bumpy rig!" he said impatiently, setting aside his curled beaver.

"You wouldn't be accustomed to the common stage, then?" the older woman asked. Curious as she was, she was made to appear more so by a pair of sharp, snuff-colored eyes that protruded inordinately from their sockets.

"No, thank God. My carriage fell into a rut and lost a wheel a mile down the road. No excuse for such wretched roads. The wheeler had nothing to fit. It could be as long as a day before . . ." The man had the distracted air of speaking to himself. He stopped midsentence and gave a weary sigh.

"You call *these* bad roads!" the pop-eyed woman declared in a disparaging way. "You ought to take the trip in early spring. A regular pothole alley. Where are you going to, then?"

He looked surprised and not pleased at the question. Unaccustomed to this low means of travel, he had no notion of the swift camaraderie that burgeoned between fellow travelers on the common stage. "Wickfield," he answered curtly, then turned to glance out the window.

"How about you, missie?" the matron continued, turning to Miss Farnsworth.

"I am going to Wickfield, too."

"There's a coincidence for you. So am I. The stage goes all the way to London. It will go empty if they don't pick up fares at Lindfield or Horsham. You're young to be racketing about the countryside alone, missie." She scrutinized Grace closely.

"I only came from Lewes, to visit my governess."

"What's her name? I know everyone at Wickfield."

Grace thought it unlikely this mushroom would know her genteel Thomas, however, and gave her name.

"Never heard of her," the woman admitted with an air of regret. "I'm Mrs. Sempleton myself. Very pleased to meet you, I'm sure. My man runs the cobbler's shop. Makes and mends boots, shoes, and slippers, and does it very well, too. He made these," she informed Grace, sticking out a sturdy shoe. "He'll fix you up in jig time if you find a sole flapping on you or a heel run down." Her bulging eyes fell to examine her companions' footgear.

Grace pulled her slippers under the seat. Her lady's slippers she had not been able to change. "My name is Jones, Grace Jones," she offered, to divert the cobbler's wife from what obviously interested her.

"You shouldn't be traveling alone, missie. But there, there'll be someone to meet you, of course?"

"Of course."

While the woman began rooting in her capacious bag, Grace turned to examine the other traveler. He was staring out the window, wearing an expression of concentration that bordered on a frown. He was not a dashing buck but handsome in a mature way. His dark hair was cropped short, his face weathered to tan. Looking at him in profile, she admired his strong nose but could not see his eyes. He seemed to be in his late thirties and had the settled, solid look of a married man. Or perhaps it was just the absence of any attractive female companionship that caused his disinterest. His jacket and boots, she noticed, while of good workmanship, did not aspire to the highest kick of fashion.

He glanced at Grace and smiled. His eyes were

5

light gray, finely lined at the edges. She thought he had a kind, understanding face. "I daresay this is your first trip alone, eh?" he asked in an avuncular tone.

"Yes, sir," she said smiling, remembering to use her high voice.

"How old are you?" he asked companionably.

"Going on thirteen, sir."

"I have a daughter your age," he told her.

The pop-eyed woman stirred, ready to rush in, and the man resumed his gaze out the window. Before long the stage drew up at a crossroads and stopped. "What the devil is going on?" he grumbled. "We're not going above five miles an hour. We'll *never* get there at this rate."

"This is where they pick up meat for the inn at Wickfield," Mrs. Sempleton informed him. She craned her neck to see half a dead cow, covered with buzzing flies, being put in the basket and covered with straw.

The man's nostrils pinched in distaste. "I must be sure not to eat at the inn," he said.

"You don't live in Wickfield, do you, Mr.—?" Mrs. Sempleton asked, impressed with his genteel disgust.

"Whewett is my name. No, I don't live there."

The protruding eyes seemed to demand more information. "Just visiting, then," she urged.

"Yes, my wife's grandmother, Lady Healy."

"I never heard of any Lady Healy in Wickfield," she told him. Her eyes held a hint of disbelief. "Me and my man have lived there fifteen years, but I never heard of any Lady Healy."

"She has not lived there for well over fifteen

6

years, and was not Lady Healy when she did. She was a Brougham by birth."

"Not one of the Broughams from Willowcrest!"

"Yes, Sir Harold's daughter."

"I knew him well. Many's the time Mr. S. has made up a pair of top boots for Sir Harold. A very long foot but narrow. A regular ruler. He's been dead many a long year, poor soul."

"Yes, Lady Healy's brother John inherited the estate. He died a few months ago," Mr. Whewett explained.

"It was the heart that took him," she agreed, nodding. "As he was a bachelor, Willowcrest belongs to this Lady Healy now, then, does it?"

"Till she disposes of it."

"You never mean Willowcrest is up for sale!" Mrs. Sempleton exclaimed, delighted to have fallen into such a wonderfully enlightening conversation.

"Not yet, but I fancy it soon will be."

"So you're married into the Broughams," the woman continued, wanting to get all details straight.

"That's right," he answered curtly, then turned to resume his gaze out the window.

Almost at once the carriage drew to a halt again, this time in front of a farmhouse. "Does this rig stop at every tree?" Whewett demanded.

"Parcel for Mrs. Gibbons," Mrs. Sempleton told him. She rolled down the window to take a good look at the box being run up the walk to the house. "Looks like a hatbox. She'd never order a hat at Lewes. It's old clothes from her sister, that's what it is. We'll get a glimpse of it in church on Sunday."

Whewett stared, too astonished to be as annoyed as he felt he should be. Her attention again turned

7

to him. "Are you making a long visit at Willow-crest, Mr. Whewett?"

"Only a day or two."

"It ain't likely we'll have the pleasure of meeting you, for Willowcrest is a good five miles from town. If you need anything in the way of a boot or shoe—"

"Yes, quite," he said, cutting her off. "I'll remember."

Mrs. Sempleton was reduced to chatting the rest of the way with a schoolgirl. "So, you're visiting your governess. Seems to me, you're young to be finished with her."

"I am not finished with her. She's on holiday."

"Seems a funny thing for a young lady to go visiting alone."

"Mama is—having a baby," Grace explained, reaching for the first excuse that came to mind.

"And the governess *would* go running off. I know just how it is. A baby, eh? Have you got any other kiddies at home?"

"No, this will be the first after me. I hope it's a boy."

"Boys are nasty things. What do you want one for?"

"Because girls talk too much," Grace answered, smiling ever so sweetly.

Mr. Whewett glanced at the girl, with the suspicion of a smile on his lips. "Tell me, Miss Jones, as you are about my daughter's age, how is your French coming along?" he inquired. "The reason I ask is that I fear Augusta, my girl, is lagging in hers."

"We have got up to subjunctives," Grace replied with a noticeable lack of enthusiasm, engendered by her memory of trying to teach the Bixworth girls.

"Already! You are doing well."

"Miss Thomas speaks French fluently."

"Is she a Frenchie?" Mrs. Sempleton demanded.

"No," Grace said, and immediately turned back to Whewett. They chatted awhile about her lessons. He found her a bright, precocious child, possessing more countenance and knowledge than Augusta. She seemed quite mature; he supposed that she had been given considerable independence. He would no more let Augusta go alone on the stage, for instance, than he would fly. Did he keep her too protected? His sister often told him so.

After another mile the conversation flagged, and he sat deep in thought. Mrs. Sempleton put her head close to Grace and whispered, "Don't take up with strange men, missie. I'll look after you if he tries anything."

The coach was small, and while Mr. Whewett did not hear all, he heard enough that, combined with Mrs. Sempleton's menacing looks, he understood her. He looked at the little girl, who glanced back with a trace of laughter in her eyes. That one silent glance established between them the realization that their traveling companion was an interfering gudgeon. For the sake of peace in the carriage Whewett paid no more attention to either female, except for an occasional surreptitious look at the girl.

She reminded him of someone—who was it? Not Irene. Was it Dolly? Yes, by God, Dolly Fraser! He hadn't thought of Doll in nearly a decade. What had happened to her? Ran off with some soldier, if memory served. He looked at the girl again, just to

9

determine she was too old to be Doll's daughter. What interested him more was the possibility that she might be *his* and Dolly's daughter. Dolores Fraser had been the toast of the tavern, his one straying from the halls of rectitude. No, certainly the girl was too old to have issued from that liaison. Indeed there was no reason to think any child had come of it. The memory of Dolly beguiled the remainder of the trip very pleasantly for him, though Mrs. Sempleton could not trust those occasional glints of interest at Miss Jones from under his half-closed eyelids.

Whewett left the carriage the instant it stopped and went to the stables to arrange the hire of a carriage. Mrs. Sempleton was surprised to see that no one met Miss Jones. Before she could express her astonishment, Miss Jones went darting down the street with her straw case in her hand, apparently knowing exactly where she was going. It looked as though the child was wearing a pair of heeled slippers. Her eyes must be failing her. As the matron puffed her way home to her rooms above the cobbler's shop, she forgot Miss Jones, but she remembered to tell Mr. S. she had met a fellow connected with the Broughams, and likely as not, Willowcrest would be up for sale soon.

"Is that so?" he asked dully. The sale of a large estate was of little interest to him, and that, too, was forgotten in the important announcement that the price of tanned leather had risen, *again.*

Chapter Two

The straw bag was heavy, and Miss Thomas's cottage well removed from the coach stop. Miss Farnsworth's arms were sore and her legs tired by the time she found the pretty rose-bordered cottage. She sighed with relief as a vision of her dear Thomas's face loomed in her mind, swiftly followed by the vision of a cup of tea and some food. Morning was long past, and breakfast had been scanty. She set the case down, gave the brass knocker two bangs, and turned the knob, planning to hop in and surprise her friend.

The knob turned half a twist, then stopped. The door was locked. She hit the knocker again, and later again, but soon realized that Miss Thomas was not at home. After thinking for a moment, she went next door to make inquiries.

"Miss Thomas?" the servant asked, frowning. "She's gone to visit relatives somewhere—a cousin feeling poorly, I believe. We're not well acquainted yet. I really couldn't say where she's gone, or for how long."

"Oh, dear!" Grace said. Her mind ran swiftly. She would have to break in and stay at Miss Thomas's cottage till she could get in touch with her.

"I'll tell you who could help you out is the couple she let the house to," the servant continued, happy to assist the child. "They'll be coming this afternoon. They will know where she is gone, likely."

"Thank you, ma'am," Grace said, her heart sinking as she walked slowly away. She went back to Thomas's doorstep and sat down to think. She couldn't even break in and stay alone. Why had not Miss Thomas let her know? The letter was probably in the mail this minute, and when it reached Bixworths', they wouldn't know where to forward it.

She was tired, hungry, and very worried, but she could not sit all day on the doorstep. She thought of her two shillings, grateful for them. She could at least have a cup of tea. Lifting the heavy case, she turned her steps back to the high street, stopping at the first tea shop she came to, for she could not carry the straw case another foot without doing permanent damage to her arm.

The establishment was more elegant than she had thought from its plain exterior. Whether even a cup of tea was within her means was doubtful. After a careful scan of the menu, she decided a child could dispense with a pourboire and used all her money to order tea and a sandwich. This done, she sat back to look at the customers. They were not particularly interesting. Mostly females in groups, taking a break from their shopping. There was one man in the corner with his nose stuck in a journal. Perhaps one of the women could tell her if anyone needed a governess. Her plan of screening her next employer flew to the winds. When her tea came, she drank and ate hungrily, then sat on, unwilling to leave the comfortable place. She had no idea where she could go.

The man in the corner put down his paper, glanced impatiently at his watch, then began to lift the paper again. He seemed to be waiting for more time to pass. He took a disinterested look around the shop before he resumed his reading. A flash of recognition lit his eyes as he spotted the girl from the stage. Odd she was alone. Whoever was to have met her had not shown up apparently. With a thought of his Augusta, he felt a rush of concern for the girl. She looked ready to burst into tears. He laid down the paper and strode over to her.

"Miss Jones, I believe?" he asked, smiling. "You remember me from the coach?"

"Oh, Mr. Whewett! Was it you hiding behind that paper all the while? I thought you would be at Willowcrest by now."

"So did I, but there's only one carriage for hire, and it won't be back till four, so I am stuck to cool my heels in town. Has something happened to your connection, too?"

A wave of despair washed over her. What had happened was so disastrous that her lower lip trembled. "I wasn't met," she confided in a troubled voice.

"I thought as much. Tell me where you want to go, and I'll take you as soon as I get my carriage. I have some hope my own may be repaired and forwarded before four o'clock."

Grace looked at him in misery and confusion. "My governess, that I was to visit, is gone," she

13

said. Despite her usual courage, she felt a warm tear start in her eye.

"Ah, that is too bad," he said, patting her hand in a kind, fatherly way that caused the tears to wash over her lids and course down her cheeks in two rivulets. A hiccup of a sob caught in her throat. "Now, you must not cry, my dear. It isn't that serious. You have only to get back home to Lewes, a mere ten miles. I'll see you onto the next stage."

"I have no money!" she sniffled.

"I'll look after it. Peculiar your governess left. Was she not expecting you?"

She shook her head in a negative. Speech was beyond her. Whewett continued, "Your mama should have made sure you were to be met, but there's no great harm after all. Come now, wipe your eyes, and I'll take you back to the inn to see when the next coach leaves."

"I can't go back there," she managed to say, trying to sniff away her tears.

"Where, to the inn?"

"No, to Lewes. I have no mother there."

Whewett sat dumbfounded. "Where is she?" he demanded.

"Dead," she answered on a fresh burst of tears.

"Did you just learn of it?" he asked, wondering how it could have happened in such an irregular fashion. The mother must have died in childbirth. He remembered some talk of Miss Jones wanting a brother. "You can go back to your papa."

"He's dead, too. I am an orphan."

"Good God!" Whewett felt a stab of pity for the poor little creature. "But my dear, you cannot stay here. Who are your family solicitors? Some relatives will come for you."

14

"Oh, you don't understand," she said, wiping her eyes with her knuckles till he stuffed his handkerchief into her fingers. She looked at his kindly, concerned face and decided on the spot she would tell him the truth. He might lend her some money to tide her over till she could find Miss Thomas.

"No, I don't understand, but I wish you will explain. I'll help you," he promised.

Grace lifted her moist eyes and looked at him hopefully. "The thing is, I am not Miss Jones at all. I am Miss Farnsworth, and I am twenty-two years old," she said.

Whewett remained perfectly impassive, except for a slight widening of his gray eyes and the lifting of one well-arched brow. He studied her young face, her hair chucked up in girlish curls, her roll-brimmed hat, and her freckles. "I begin to think you are a minx, Miss Whoever-You-Are. Now, let us hear the truth, if you please, without benefit of a Cheltenham tragedy. Have you run away from school? Is that it?"

Her chin lifted pugnaciously, which only increased the air of youthful rebellion. "School is closed in August."

"You have peeled away from home in any case, or I miss my bet. You have run yourself to a standstill, so there is no need of a lecture. I wager you are ready to go home and face the music."

"I told you, I *have* no home," she said, becoming impatient.

For ten minutes she spoke on, explaining in detail her predicament. Her voice, no longer pitched childishly high, her vocabulary, her whole conduct, soon convinced him of the truth. "This is almost

15

worse than your first story," he said, sinking his chin in his hands to look at her in astonishment.

"I know that! The question is, what am I to do?" Her voice held a note of desperation.

Whewett continued studying her, silently now. The idea that had just cropped into his head was so outré, he could hardly believe it had even occurred to him. He was not a gentleman who routinely involved himself in drama of any sort. The even tenor of his days was seldom disturbed by anything more interesting than politics or domestic doings.

Yet, as he considered it, he found his scheme not only possible but fairly easy to execute. Miss Farnsworth passed very well for a young girl, and what he needed at that moment was a girl of the age she appeared. "Come with me," he said.

Grace blinked in surprise. "To Willowcrest?"

"Yes, I need you."

"What on earth for?"

"To be my daughter."

An air of withdrawal settled on her. "You already have a daughter," she pointed out stiffly.

"I don't have her here."

"What has that to do with it?"

"A great deal. Let me explain. Lady Healy was my wife's grandmother."

Grace, listening closely, discerned an inconsistency in his first speech. *"Was?* Surely she is not dead. You said you were going to visit her."

"Ah, no, my wife is dead. Lady Healy is alive and kicking. She has come down from Scotland to see about being rid of Willowcrest. She is old, in her seventies, and not at all well. She has never seen Augusta and is eager to do so. It would mean a good deal to her."

16

"Then why did you not bring your daughter with you?"

"She is out of the country. Lady Healy will think she is seeing her when she sees you. I ought to warn you, she is a—trifle eccentric."

"If you mean she is a raving lunatic, pray say so," Grace said sternly.

A small smile parted his lips, to hear such authority issue from what appeared to be a child's mouth. "You will find I say what I mean. She is a trifle eccentric, no more, Miss Jones."

"My name is Farnsworth."

"So you say." Her chin jutted forth, but he spoke on before she could challenge him. "I don't blame you for lying to that wretched woman. I lied myself."

"If you are not Mr. Whewett, pray who are you?"

"Mr. Dalmy, but it would be more proper to call me Lord Whewett."

Grace was overcome with new doubts. She had never known a lord to hide his light under a bushel, but for a commoner to assume a handle to his name was nothing new. "You don't look like a lord."

His head rose, his nostrils pinched, and he said "Indeed!" in what Grace concluded could only be a noble fit of pique. "I am Lord Whewett, not that it is either here or there. About Lady Healy—she is not only eccentric, but very rich. It has been the custom in the family for the wife's portion to go to the daughter. Lady Healy has managed to outlive both her daughter and grandaughter. If she doesn't outlive my Augusta as well, her fortune will go to her. Lady Healy has expressed, rather imperatively, a desire to see her heir. Augusta was on holiday in Ireland with my sister when the summons

17

came. As Lady Healy makes only a short visit, it is impossible to get Augusta back in time."

"Why do you not just tell her so?"

"You have, no doubt, heard the old cliché, 'Oh, what a tangled web we weave . . .' I have been lying to Lady Healy for years. She has often asked me to send Augusta to her in Scotland. First I made the excuse she was too young to travel, because I did not want to subject the poor child to such an ordeal. Augusta is shy, and Grandma Healy is—how shall I say it? She is autocratic, self-centered, a grande dame of the old school. She would frighten my Gussie to death, so I invented a weak constitution for my daughter. To hear Augusta is well enough to have jauntered off to Ireland might cause Lady Healy to settle the estate elsewhere for spite. I do not wish to lose my daughter her inheritance because of my doings. The money belongs to Augusta by rights, and I mean to see she gets it. I had intended to claim my daughter had taken a turn for the worse. It would be infinitely preferable if I could produce a daughter."

"You have chosen your new daughter poorly, sir. I do not have a frail constitution."

"Her grandmother will be delighted at the improvement. I receive long screeds of suggested treatments. You might claim a headache or upset stomach during the visit," he suggested.

Grace felt her interest rising, almost in spite of herself. "What does your daughter look like?" she asked.

"That does not matter. Lady Healy's never seen her."

Grace was shocked at the lapse. "Have you not even sent her a picture?"

"Yes, of a three-year-old Augusta. Your coloring is not so different, except that Gussie has blue eyes. She is thinner, too. You are not so very unlike my late wife. You could pass for her daughter."

Grace felt her fears lessen at this description. So long as Whewett considered her strictly as a daughter, the visit was possible. At two and twenty, she was not unaware of the impropriety and danger implicit in the scheme of a widower and an unmarried lady traveling together. "Would it not be illegal?" she asked, frowning.

"I don't know. I did not think that would bother *you*."

She bristled. "I am not a *criminal*, Lord Whewett!"

"Not an inveterate one, I'm sure, but you can hardly be unaware it is illegal to defraud the coaching company of half their fare by posing as a child." This was said in no threatening way, but Grace thought she detected a hint of blackmail. Her hackles were up at once.

"It was a case of the direst necessity!"

"Just so. I have no intention of reporting you. If you do not choose to oblige me, I shall still help you—lend you money or take you somewhere. One can hardly abandon a lady in such distress. I don't plan to use coercion, but you must see your case could hardly be worse, Miss Farnsworth. You are destitute, with no friend to turn to. You have nothing to lose, whereas I have a fortune to lose for my daughter. The risk is ninety-nine percent my own. I wouldn't take it if I were not sure of success. Who is there to find us out? You know no one in the village except Miss Thomas, and she, one assumes, would hardly reveal your secret. We will only be

19

here for a couple of days. There will be no need to leave Willowcrest at all. And of course I shall reward you handsomely for your acting chore," he added temptingly.

"How much?" As he spoke, she had listened closely, and acknowledged the truth of what he said. Now she listened to hear the reward.

"What do you figure it is worth?"

"I've no idea. I never did anything like this before. Mrs. Bixworth pays a hundred pounds a year."

"I'll give you a hundred for two days."

"Oh, no! That is too much!"

"My daughter stands to gain something in the neighborhood of fifty thousand."

"I see," Grace said weakly. "Then it is *not* too much. But still, I don't know if I could do it. How can I, at my age, act like a child for forty-eight hours?"

Whewett hunched his elegant shoulders and smiled. "You fooled me. You fooled the coachman. You fooled that bug-eyed old nosey parker on the coach with us. I fancy, if you pulled the wool over *her* eyes, you will have no trouble fooling Grandma Healy. She is not so sharp-eyed these days."

"I found it a dreadful strain to pitch my voice high, like a girl, and to remember to call everyone sir or ma'am."

He flicked an atom of dust from his coat sleeve. "A hundred and fifty pounds, to cover the additional strain."

"I'm not after more money," she said with an air of offense. "The payment first offered is generous. I must think about it a moment."

She crossed her arms, sat back very straight, with an expression of fierce concentration on her young face. Whewett watched with bated breath while she swiftly passed the pros and cons through review and took her decision. "I'll do it," she announced.

He breathed a vast sigh of relief. "Good girl! You won't be sorry."

They reached across the table and shook hands, smiling uncertainly. Having formed an alliance put them both in a happier mood. Grace, left light with relief that at least she knew where she would lay her head that night, would have a hundred pounds when the job was done, which seemed a fortune to her.

"I expect the next step is to get me some children's clothing," she said. "I have my skirt rolled around half a dozen times and require something more suitable. Grandma Healy—you see how quickly I am coming along—will expect Lady Augusta to wear something better than a shiny serge suit two years old. I'll need a round bonnet, too, and flat-heeled shoes. It was the slippers I feared would give me away on the coach. I daresay you did not notice, but these are ladies' slippers I am wearing."

"On the contrary, I always notice a lady's ankles," he replied unceremoniously. "Even a young lady's. I thought yours showed definite promise. Now, where shall we pick up these items you require?"

Grace blinked in surprise, but answered his question. "It will have to be a dress already made, if we're lucky. Do you trust me to do it alone, or are you afraid I'll take your money and skip?"

"I'll take the chance." He drew out a fat purse and began peeling off bills. "Here's fifteen pounds. Is it enough?"

"That's three times more than I shall need."

"Take it all—a gift, no strings attached. If you want to, you can outfit yourself for our masquerade and meet me at the inn. If you change your mind, you can hop the next coach to wherever you like. I shan't have you followed. Fair enough?"

Grace shook her head ruefully. "You know I can't shab off when you make such a handsome offer."

"I trust you are a gentleman, in affairs of business. I shall be at the inn at four. If my carriage is not there by then, I shall hire one and go on to Willowcrest. I told Lady Healy today. She does not like being balked."

"Does she expect you to have your daughter with you?"

"She told me to bring her. I didn't reply, but came on to make my excuses in person."

"No reason she should be looking for any tricks, then. Did you plan all along to hire a daughter?"

"No, that would have required a trip to London. It was your sad tale that put the notion in my head. It almost seemed like fate, our meeting so felicitously."

"It was a happy chance for me as well. I'll be at the inn at four. Good-bye, Mr. Whewett."

"I'll take your case with me." He rose and bowed gracefully. "*Au revoir*, Miss Farnsworth."

She rose and began to walk away, then stopped and looked back over her shoulder. She thought he was looking at her ankles. "I should have said *Lord* Whewett!"

His flashing smile might almost have been called a grin. "You should have said Papa, Doll." Her eyes widened at such a familiar form of address. His expression softened. "It is what I call my daughter," he lied easily. "A pet name, you might say. Be good.

22

Don't go talking to strangers." A low chuckle followed her as she hurried out of the tea shop.

Despite her gentlemanly instincts, Grace considered quite seriously bolting on Lord Whewett. He said the money was a gift, so she was free to do as she liked. Was he trustworthy? He had told his story quite frankly on the stage, only omitting that he was a lord. A man bent on mischief would not have done so. Mrs. Sempleton had corroborated his story—she knew the Broughams. He had been sincere in trying to help her when he thought her a child. Likely he still thought of her as a child. He was a father, a solid, sensible gentleman. Except that he had come up with the outrageous idea for this masquerade. And he had noticed her ankles and called her Doll in a way that did not sound at all fatherly. Oh, what *should* she do?

Only two days out of her boring life. What did it matter? There was no real harm in it, and if trouble *did* arise, Lord Whewett must protect her to protect himself. Lords were practically impervious to legal proceedings. The worst she could envisage was that Lady Healy should somehow discover their trick and send her packing. She would have her money in even less than two days.

How fine it would be to have a hundred pounds! She decided to go through with it and spent the afternoon shopping. She was very careful to call all the clerks sir. Every one of them mentioned it was odd her being alone. She invented the story that her mama was waiting in the carriage. She had taken a dizzy spell. No one questioned her story when they saw her money.

At a quarter to four she walked up to the inn door, her arms full of parcels. Standing in the yard

23

was the most elegant black chaise she had ever seen, with a crest on its side and four shiny bays in the harness. A footman wearing green livery hopped down and bowed to her.

"Allow me, Lady Augusta," he said, taking her parcels with a sly wink. Lord Whewett had been busy to inform his servants of the charade. Funny, she had thought just the two of them would be involved in it. It was a more elaborate affair than she had envisaged.

The proprietor held the door for her and bowed till his nose very nearly touched his protruding stomach. "His lordship is waiting for you in his private parlor, milady. I hope you'll be comfortable," he said, and held the door wide for her to enter.

Whewett sat before a window looking over his journal. He rose when she entered. "Hallo, Gussie. How did the shopping go? A pity your woman could not have accompanied you. I trust there was no trouble?"

"No trouble, Papa," she answered, scarcely able to hold her lips steady, for the whole business was so very strange. Servants and innkeepers bobbing to her, and a lord standing up when she entered the room, while she was rigged out like a child.

"Put Lady Augusta's parcels there, Hucker," Whewett directed the footman. "Would you like a cup of tea before we leave, Augusta?"

"Yes, please," she replied happily. The bottle of wine at his elbow also interested her.

The proprietor bowed and left, closing the door behind him. "You'd ought to have let me go with the lass. It looked odd-like for her to be on the streets alone and hauling her own bags and boxes," Hucker said.

"I'm sure Miss Farnsworth lent even that a touch of plausibility," Whewett replied. "How did it really go?" he asked, turning to Grace.

"Fine. I got everything I need and have money left."

"Keep it. Mad money. I had Hucker pick you up a decent light traveling case. That is—" He came to a conscious stop, glancing to see if the lady had taken offense.

Hucker produced a leather case bound in brass. "That was well thought of," she replied nonchalantly. "What shall I do with the indecent one I brought with me?"

"We'll discard it here. You will want its contents put into the new one, for when the play is over."

"Yes. Are all your servants in on the scheme?"

"Just me, Trudgen, the groom and my valet, Jenner." Hucker replied.

"You may leave us now, Hucker," Whewett said. The footman left. "I had to tell them," he added. "They know you're not Gussie. They are to be trusted implicitly. Indeed, they are enjoying themselves hugely. Of course I told them nothing of your personal history."

"I am not ashamed of it!" she said sharply, pulling open the straw case to repack her belongings.

"No reason you should be. It is hardly your fault that your father was improvident. There are a good many things you need to know. We live at Downsfield, outside of Dover, not far removed from the coast. You and I live alone but for the servants. Your governess is Miss Invers, a good woman. I don't know if Lady Healy is familiar with the name. I have a sister, Mary, married to Lord Dewitt, from Ireland, where they make their home."

25

"That is where your real daughter is now?"

"From this moment *you* are my real daughter. The Dewitts spend the season in London. They have two girls, Catharine and Anne, aged seven and six respectively. You know them fairly well from their visits to us. If embarrassing questions arise, I'll try to give you a hand. Grandma Healy is not intimately aware of our business, which is all to the good. She was my wife's grandmother, and since her death, she takes little enough interest in me."

"Who are you? I mean what kind of lord?"

"Tory, of course."

"I mean your rank. Are you a baron—"

"An earl."

"I should know your Christian name, too."

"Alfred, and yours is Augusta Isabel, the Augusta after Grandma Healy. Don't forget it."

"Don't call me Doll, then, or she won't like it. What about my mother? Did I know her at all?"

"She died ten years ago. You would have no recollection of her. Her name was Irene. She was your type, generally speaking. Small. Not so small as you, quite, but smallish, with brown hair."

Grace finished the packing and went to sit beside him. The tea tray was brought in by an obsequious servant. It was amusing to watch him bow and truckle to Whewett and treat her with that combination of respect and playfulness deemed suitable to a noble child. As soon as they were alone, the lesson continued.

"You enjoy riding. No matter if you don't really. There will be no occasion to do so at Willowcrest. You have not traveled at all."

"What of cousins and so on that I should know about?"

26

"None on the Brougham side. She would have no interest in any others. Oh, hell!" A quick frown pinched his brows together. "She and Augusta correspond once a month. I don't know what is in the letters. Fake it if you can."

Instructions and facts were poured out in such a rapid stream, Grace did not grasp the half of them, but she did her best. When tea was finished, she said, "Should we not be getting along?"

"No hurry. The later we arrive, the less time you'll have to be with her. It will be a strain on you, I imagine."

"I'm worried sick," she confessed. "What if I make a shambles of it?"

"You won't. I'll be there to give you a hand. I'll try not to leave you alone with her. And Miss Farnsworth," he added in a hopeful voice, "be nice to her. She will not be easy to be nice to, but it would be a shame if anything should arise to turn her against my daughter."

Grace saw the worry etching lines on his forehead and felt a spasm of pity for Whewett. Whatever else he was, he was certainly a considerate father. "I'll try. There is just one thing—why did we not bring Invers with us?"

"Good point. We'll say her mother is ill, and she had gone home to Sussex for a week. Invers is actually in Ireland with Gussie, of course."

"I feel as if I had a herd of stampeding horses in my stomach. If anything goes wrong, what becomes of me? She'll throw me out on my ear."

"Us, on our collective ear. We're in this together. If you give any wrong answers, I shall claim you're addlepated from the trip. Gussie doesn't travel, remember?"

She straightened her shoulders, lifted her chin, and said in her new childish voice, "Don't you think it is time to leave, Papa?"

"Yes, Doll." When he cocked his head to one side and laughed, he looked ten years younger and much more attractive. "What's the matter?" he demanded, seeing her studious gaze.

"You were to call me Augusta because of its being Grandma's name," she reminded him.

"I'll try to remember," he said, and went to the door to call Hucker to take out the luggage.

As Grace left the room with Whewett behind her, she had an instinctive feeling he was looking at her ankles. They almost tingled from the imagined perusal. She was struck with a terrible premonition of disaster and had to force herself to advance sedately to the carriage.

Chapter Three

A five-mile trip in a well-sprung chaise bore no resemblance to a ten-mile one on the common stage. As Grace was wafted along the road, she admired the blue velvet squabs and the elegant silver appointments of the interior. The trip was over before it seemed possible and before Grace felt quite ready to become Lady Augusta. "Chin up," Whewett said, offering his arm as she descended from the carriage.

Till she was striding along beside him toward the house, she had not realized he was so very tall. Besides having to reach up to hold his arm, it was necessary to lengthen her stride uncomfortably, for he did not shorten his. She took only a glance at the building she was entering. It was a sprawling redbrick place, more wide than high. The lengthening shadows of evening emphasized the unkempt condition of both grounds and house. Though there were no Gothic windows or brooding elms, it struck

Grace as the proper setting for a Gothic novel. The brick was not perishing, but dusty windows and overgrown grass caused the proper air of brooding menace.

The servant who showed them in was a groom masquerading as a butler and looked it. His rough manner and ill-fitting jacket suited the house, however. Lady Healy had come to a place that had been standing empty for some time, and she had only her own few servants to tend to it.

"You'd be his lordship," the servant said. "Come in, then. She's been waiting forever." He sounded put upon as he pointed a peremptory and not very clean finger toward a lighted saloon.

It was in this ghastly Purple Saloon, large and dingy, with the fading sun filtering through dusty glass and dispirited lace curtains, that Grace had her first view of her new grandmother. Whewett had called the dame old, leading her to expect a decrepit little gray-haired lady with a humped back. What stood glaring at her was a positive grenadier with jet black hair, heavy black brows, a mannish hooked nose, and a scowl. She wore a stylish black silk gown trimmed with bugle beads, while her bodice sparkled with diamonds. The gnarled fingers clutching a blackthorn walking stick were cluttered with rings.

"About time you got here!" was the harridan's opening salvo, fired off in a rough voice. "Well, come into the light, child, and let us have a look at you."

Grace felt a nearly uncontrollable urge to turn and flee out the front door. She clung to Whewett's arm, till he gave her a nudge forward into the puddle of light emanating from a table lamp. With her clear brown eyes goggling and her lip fallen a little

30

open in fright, she looked young enough that Whewett had no fear of instant disclosure.

"Humph. Turn around," the dame ordered. In instant obedience, Grace turned slowly. "She didn't get the Brougham looks, more's the pity. Nor yours, either, Whewett. Takes after her maternal grandfather—well, after her mama, if it comes to that. Dumpy little thing. Mousy hair, no countenance. I hope you ain't a saucy chit, are you?"

"N-no, ma'am," Grace answered in a cowed voice.

"Not a *blancmanger*, either. I have no use for *blancmangers*. Do you stand up for yourself, eh?"

"Yes, ma'am," Grace answered, turning an appealing eye to Whewett, who threw himself into the breach.

"Grandma, you have not made me welcome. Do I not get a kiss after my trip to see you?" He stepped forward for the greeting.

"Ha. You ought to be able to do better than an old relict like me. Come here and kiss me, then, if you insist." She turned her cheek to receive the kiss, but did not return it. Her main interest was still on Grace.

"How about you, Augusta? Have you got a kiss for your old grandmother?"

Grace dutifully stood on tiptoe and reached up to do her duty. As the initial shock of the meeting subsided, Grace noticed that at close range the lady was indeed ancient. From pride in her appearance perhaps, she had placed herself in a dim light, but her cheeks were etched with lines, while those eyes that looked like coals from across the room were bleared with age. Her whole aspect was forbidding. Grace felt a start of terror when the old woman put both arms around her and hugged her. She felt as

31

though she had been snatched up by an eagle and felt, too, an instinctive urge to fight free. But this was supposed to be her beloved grandmother. With a conscious effort of will, she stood still and even returned the embrace.

"There! You ain't afraid of me, are you?" the old lady asked, releasing her. Staring in fascination, Grace saw a tear glistening on that raddled cheek.

Her fear and revulsion softened to pity. "Grandma, how should I be afraid of you?" she asked, smiling.

"Ah, she's a fine gal, a bonnie lass," Lady Healy decreed, turning to Whewett. Mousiness, dumpiness, all were forgiven at such a slim indication of love.

"Indeed she is. I am very proud of her," he replied in the accents of a fond father.

"Let us all sit down and be comfortable," Lady Healy suggested. "We shall have some wine before dinner. Wretched stuff old John had laid in. He had no taste; never had. No wine for you, missie. Till your hair is up and you are into long skirts, you get no wine. I hope you ain't feeding her wine, Alfred?"

"No, Augusta does not drink wine."

"A glass of lemonade. I had them make you up some lemonade. Brought the lemons with me from Scotland. You may think we are savages in the north, but I have six lemon trees in my orangery. You will like lemonade, eh, Augusta?"

"That will be lovely, thank you."

"Wine stunts the growth, you must know. Not one drop was I permitted till I was sixteen. My brothers were into it before they were fourteen and were not an inch taller than myself. John was shorter, though he put wedges in his boots to hide

32

it. Your growth don't want stunting, Augusta. You are going to be squat, like your mama."

"Irene was not squat," Whewett objected.

"She was a squab, Whewett, and if you had not been blinded by love, you would have known what a sight the two of you looked together, like a kitten and a bear. No matter. Augusta is young yet. She will grow a couple of inches. I want you to grow at least three inches, Gussie. I was called Gussie when I was young. It sounds like a bruiser. I daresay they call you that name, too."

"Sometimes," Grace answered carefully.

"I suppose you have lots of friends at Downsfield?"

"Some friends," she said vaguely. This point had not been covered in the sketchy lesson.

"How about that silly girl you told me of in your last letter? Did she get her tooth that was bothering her drawn?"

"Sally's tooth fell out before it was necessary, didn't it, Gussie?" Whewett mentioned casually.

"Yes," Grace said, taking it up eagerly. "She was relieved. No one likes going to the tooth drawer."

"Rubbish. I never minded having a tooth drawn when I was young," Lady Healy told them. "I am seventy-five years old and still have my own teeth. Not so white as they used to be, and jiggling loose at the back of my mouth the half of them, but they're all there, and they're all mine. Do you brush your teeth every night, Gussie?"

"Certainly I do, Grandma."

"You have a nice set of teeth. Not so white as mine were. Take care of them. There is nothing ruins a girl's looks like a set of brown or yellow teeth. They have a good many yellow teeth in Scotland.

33

They wear well, the yellow ones. With your mousy hair, Augusta, you will want all the help good teeth can give you to make you pretty."

"Actually," Whewett pointed out, "Gussie's hair is chestnut, not mousy."

"Looks mousy in this demmed dim light. We want another brace of candles. John was so cheap, I could find nothing but tallow candles. They have a stench. Never mind, we'll be going to dinner soon. I am famished. I daresay you two are as well. You are eating with the grown-ups tonight, Gussie, as a special treat. For once it won't spoil you. I hope you don't have her at the adult table at Downsfield, Alfred?"

"Not for dinner. We take breakfast and lunch together. If I have no company in the evening, Gussie joins me."

Grace listened closely to learn what she could of her imaginary past life. "It is lonesome eating alone," Lady Healy said. "Since Willie up and died on me, I have been alone but for old Mulkins, my companion. A gudgeon. I sent her off to her room to be rid of her. Well now, let us all get acquainted. I want to hear all about your life, Augusta."

"How long do you propose staying at Willowcrest, Grandma?" Whewett asked rather quickly, to divert the lady's interest.

The adults sipped their wine, while the alleged child drank her lemonade. "Only a short visit," she told him. "As I said in my letter to you, I wanted to see the old place before selling it off. There is no point holding on to it, but I shall pick up a few mementos of the old days and decide what price to ask for it. You can help me there, Alfred."

"I will be happy to, but I can't stay long."

"I know you can never spare two days in a row, but it won't take two days to ride around with the bailiff and see what kind of decay John has let the place fall into. Gone to rack and ruin like the house, I make no doubt. This used to be a handsome place. I cannot think who had the saloon hung in purple, like a state funeral. Your visit will give Augusta and me a chance to get to know each other. We'll like that, eh, Gussie? Just the two of us. You can tell me all about your lessons and friends and horses. Are you a bruising rider?"

Grace new Augusta rode, and said, "Papa says I am good."

"Do you ride a real horse or a pony?"

"A horse," she said, as some reply must be made.

"I got a bay mare for Gussie a year ago," Whewett added.

"Good! Excellent! Do you hunt, Augusta?"

Grace glanced to Whewett, who shook his head slightly. "Not yet, Grandma, but I hope to soon."

"I was hunting when I was ten. I was a big girl for my age. Don't dally. Don't be frightened, just because you took that tumble a few months ago. Everyone takes a spill now and then. It is half the fun of riding."

"It wasn't serious," Whewett remarked. "No bones broken."

"How did it happen?" the lady asked, throwing Grace into alarm.

"Augusta was never much good at ditches," he said, giving Grace a lead.

"I wasn't hurt much," she ventured.

"A ditch is fine, soft falling. I never minded tumbling into a ditch, unless it was full of water," Lady Healy said, then mercifully turned her attention to

35

the father to grill him on other matters. When dinner was announced, the masquerade was still successful.

Grace was sorry to see no wine glass at her place, but at least there was a large meal that promised to satisfy even her appetite.

"You're a good trencherman," the grandmother congratulated, which led Grace to believe she might request a second helping.

"No seconds, Augusta," Lady Healy said. "You dumpy little girls don't want to be taking seconds, or you'll run to fat before you make your bows. You must watch every pound. If you were a ladder like myself, you might have as many seconds as you please. Put another slice of that ham on my plate, Whewett. There's a good lad. Don't allow your daughter seconds, or snacks between meals, either. If she is like her mama, she'll be stuffing herself with sugarplums and marchpane every time she goes to town. Irene hadn't time to spread before she died, but she was destined to run to fat."

Grace looked forlornly at the plate of viands of which she could have no more and waited eagerly for dessert. She was permitted a pear and a piece of cheese, and as it was a special occasion, her grandma allowed her one macaroon to celebrate. An apple tart passed her by while her cook's skill with this particular dessert was expounded upon. "Nutmeg and cinnamon, and plenty of sugar. My, don't it smell delicious!" The old dame cleaned her plate quickly and passed it along for another slice.

Watching Grace follow every bite with her eyes, Whewett said, "Don't you think we might let Augusta have a piece on this special day?"

"She had a macaroon. Don't spoil her. We must

be cruel to be kind. Don't let her wrap you round her finger, Alfred. She'll tow the line here as at home."

Whewett shrugged an apology across the table at Grace. After dinner he was invited in a commanding way to bring his port to the saloon and did so. He was about to pour a glass when Lady Healy said, "Time for you to leave us, young lady. I do not approve of children in the saloon after dinner."

Grace looked startled, for it was only eight o'clock. "Where shall I go?" she asked.

"To your bed, of course," Lady Healy replied.

"But it's only—!" Grace intercepted a look from Whewett and fell silent.

"I see how it is. Your papa lets you stay up till all hours. It will destroy your looks. Dims the eyes and make the skin sallow. Young girls should rise with the sun and retire with it. By the time you have cleaned your teeth and said your prayers and changed, it will be close to nine o'clock. I notice your woman did not come with you. Don't you have an abigail, Gussie?"

"Miss Invers has gone to visit her family. Her mother is ill," Grace replied.

"All the more reason to run along. You'll have to do for yourself. It will be a lesson in independence."

"I can take care of myself," Grace said, feeling this bold assertion might meet with approval, as indeed it did.

"I wager you can," the old lady cackled merrily.

When Grace went to make her curtsy to her grandmother, the lady said, "You may kiss me good-night, Gussie."

With no inner revulsion this time, Grace pecked the sere, lined skin. She turned uncertainly toward

Whewett, wondering in what manner she ought to take her leave of him. "Good night, Papa," she said, and curtsied.

"Good night, Augusta. Sleep well," he answered, with a glint of amusement at her predicament.

"Don't you kiss your father good-night?" Lady Healy asked. Her tone made it perfectly clear she did not approve of a mere curtsy.

Not wishing to give offense, Grace said, "Sometimes."

"You should always kiss your father good-night. There isn't enough respect shown to parents nowadays. My father would have laid a hickory branch over my back if I forgot to kiss him good-night. Don't forget to brush your teeth and say your prayers, too."

"Yes, Grandmama," Grace answered, her voice becoming strained at all these commands. She turned to Whewett, glowering at him when her back was safely turned from Lady Healy.

"Come and kiss your father good-night as you're told," he said in a fatherly way.

She walked to him stiffly. "Beast!" she hissed in a low voice as her lips brushed his cheek. The roughness of incipient whiskers surprised her. At close range a lingering hint of spicy cologne rose from him. It surprised her, too, when he reached out and grasped her wrist in his hand.

"Sleep tight, dear. I'll look in on you before I go to bed. We shan't be staying up late, Grandma?"

The old dame yawned. "I am dog-tired already. We'll turn in soon. We have only got the east wing open. I have had you two put in adjoining rooms for company. I have only a handful of servants with me. One of them will show you where to go, Augusta."

Grace's eyes flew to Whewett in consternation at the sleeping arrangements. "How convenient." He smiled blandly at Lady Healy.

"I knew you would like to be close together," she said.

Grace was shown to a large chamber of faded elegance by the groom-turned-butler. "This here's where you're sleeping," was his sole conversation.

Dark wainscoting and dark window hangings lent a dismal atmosphere to the whole. In lieu of a proper lamp, there was one brace of tallow candles to lighten the heavy gloom and disperse a rancid smoke. Her new luggage sat on the floor, unpacked. Stowing it away took a few minutes.

By eight-thirty she was done, stuck in a shadowy room alone, already half-hungry, and unlikely to close her eyes before midnight. There was nothing to read, nothing to do, no one to talk to. She flung herself on the lumpy bed to wait till it got late enough to really think of retiring. She would not undress till Whewett came. She reviewed the strange day, which had such unusual happenings that the time passed without tedium. At nine there was a tap at the adjoining door. She ran to open it.

Whewett stood on the other side, smiling. "You were marvelous, Doll," he congratulated her, and stepped in with no hesitation, nor much feeling of strangeness.

"Thank you. It didn't go too badly, but I am happy it is only a short visit. I do not look forward with any pleasure to being sent to my room at eight o'clock. Even at Bixworths', I was allowed up till ten."

"She shipped me off at nine, not much better."

"Will we have to stay all day tomorrow?"

"I'm afraid so. We've been discussing that below-stairs. She wants me to ride over the place and speak to the estate manager she's been dealing with since her arrival. It will take a few days more."

"A few days more! Whewett, you said two days altogether. I thought today was one of them."

"We were not here today," he pointed out reasonably. "She wants to see more of you than that."

"Two more nights locked in this dungeon! You must get me some books and some decent lights. And something to eat. I am starved."

"Sorry about the apple tart. You must own I tried, but you dumpy girls, you know . . ."

"I am not dumpy. I am petite," Grace sniffed. "There is a difference."

"I noticed but did not think it wise to call the difference to Grandma's attention. Are you actually hungry?"

"No, I am actually starved. I had a cup of tea for breakfast, and exactly one thin sandwich for luncheon."

Whewett looked uncertain. "I have a box of bonbons I picked up for my housekeeper. You may have them if you promise to clean your teeth."

"I promise to clean the box, in any case." He made no move to get the bonbons. "Oh, of course I'll clean my teeth. I'm twenty-two years old, not a child."

"It's easy to forget," he said, glancing at her short skirts. The gown had a loose, smock-type top that concealed her figure.

Whewett went to his room and returned with the box of bonbons, which he opened to pass to her before selecting one himself. "Revolting, aren't they?" he asked, chewing without the least sign of pleasure.

"They are delicious! Try the little round one. It has a cherry in liqueur." He laid the box aside. "Do you think you should go? I mean, in case she comes," Grace added.

"Don't worry. I'm not going to eat any more of your candy. As to Grandma's coming, there is nothing wrong with my talking to my daughter, and while you are in this house, Dolly, you are my daughter. Don't forget it."

"I'm not likely to, with Lady Healy asking me every minute if I remembered to dry behind my ears."

"She's sharp-tongued, but she likes you immensely. She had a dozen compliments the minute you left. This was an excellent idea, bringing you here. It is giving her so much pleasure, it would be a shame to deprive her of it. Augusta would not have done half so well herself. A shy child like Gussie would have been terrified of the old Tartar, but you did excellently. How did you get so brave?"

"From dealing with Mrs. Bixworth, who is enough of a terror to frighten Lady Healy. I think Grandma is really lonesome beneath her rough exterior. There was a tear on her cheek when I kissed her, Whewett. Did you notice it?"

"Yes, but it was a tear of joy, I think."

"I hope so." Grace unthinkingly put another chocolate in her mouth and chewed. "Everyone's lonesome underneath, I imagine. Even you."

"*Even* I? Widows and widowers are more lonesome than most. So lonesome, I deserve another bonbon," he decided, and popped one in his mouth.

"They can't be more lonesome than orphans," she pointed out with a sad look.

"Pity we don't have a couple of violins to back up this threnody," he said, and passed her the bonbons.

"I'm worried about being alone with her tomorrow while you're out. God only knows what she will ask me."

"The blessing is that if she asks you, it means she doesn't know herself. All we have to do is get together and compare notes later so I don't contradict what you tell her. It seems fairly inconsequential stuff that interests her. Do you ride, by the way?"

"I used to when Papa was alive, but I did not begin hunting when I was ten. Do you believe half her stories?"

"Yes, I would say I believe half of them. She had the reputation of being quite a terror in her youth. I expect we drop the less glorious memories as we advance into old age."

"I hope so."

"What memories do you plan to dump?" he asked, regarding her closely. From what he knew of her thus far, he could not think of anything she would want to remember.

"This job for one. My last for another."

"I've been so busy telling you all the circumstances and history of the Whewett house that I've had very little time to learn about you. How long have you been an orphan, Miss Farnsworth?"

"A year and a few months. It seems much longer."

"Have you been a governess all that time?"

"No, for six months I lived in a fool's paradise at

home with Thomas. It took that long to straighten out Papa's accounts and discover I was in the basket. It came as such a shock. Then I battened myself quite shamelessly on Miss Thomas for a few months in a little apartment she had rented, till I got a job and she moved here. I haven't seen her since, but we correspond regularly. I cannot imagine where she went without letting me know."

"What an awful time you have had," he said, shaking his head in sympathy. "Now to cap it off, you are all but abducted to perform a masquerade under the most harrowing circumstances. Have you no relatives you might go to?"

"I have some cousins, but I don't know them well and dislike to be dependent on others."

"I'm sure they would be charmed to have you."

She flashed a sharp eye at that. "They none of them asked me, and they knew I was alone."

"You could have asked them," he said reasonably.

"You mean go *begging*! Pride is a bad trait for one in my circumstances, but—"

"Let us call it by its other name, self-respect, which is a good trait in anyone. I had thought you would be closer to your extended family."

"No, I hardly knew them. Well, here it is nearly nine-thirty. Time for me to turn in."

"To what?" he inquired with a lazy smile. "A princess? Your sad tale calls to mind Perrault's *Cinderella*."

"No, that would require a prince, I believe."

Whewett shrugged, trying to lighten her morose mood. "And our Prinney doesn't even care for slender young ladies. He prefers more bulk, preferably with a touch of silver hair. Good night, Augusta. I haven't the heart to remind you to brush your teeth," he said, rising to go toward the door.

Grace went with him to bolt the door. She stopped with an exclamation of surprise. "There is no lock!"

He looked down, then at the other side of the door. "I'm safe. There's one on my side."

The door silently closed behind him, and the bolt was drawn. Grace frowned a moment, but soon began to undress. Not a single fear for her safety came into her head. Her only concern was for the morning, and what new unpleasantness it might bring. But really, it had not been so bad. She was no longer afraid of Lady Healy, and any small misgivings as to Whewett's respectability were long past. She was soon in bed, and before long, deep peaceful breaths filled the chamber.

Chapter Four

Grace was not quite up with the sun, but she rose not much after it. A country servant, younger than Grace herself and pretty in a robust way, came and shook her awake. "Time to get up, missie," she said gaily. "Your grandma is up and wants me to do your hair."

Grace rubbed her eyes as she looked around the strange room. The brown walls of the preceding evening had softened to a faded yellow, with lighter spots that might, perhaps, be roses. The sunlight streaming through the dusty panes picked out heavy mahogany furnishings from a past era. Memory returned, causing her to look in alarm at the servant. Grace got out of bed and turned toward the window to scramble into her dress, to prevent the girl's discovering she was not a child. Once the concealing dress was on, she felt safer. The servant took a brush to her hair, yanking it hard, then pulling it into two tails, with a part down the back.

"My name's Molly," the servant said as she worked. "This here is how I do my sister's hair."

As Molly stuck two large blue bows on the ends of the braids, Grace glanced in the mirror and felt she was looking at a veritable youngster. If ever she had to pass as a minor again, she'd know how to accomplish it. "Thank you," she said in a voice strangled with suppressed laughter.

Whewett's lips twitched in amusement when she appeared in the breakfast parlor. "A new style, Augusta?" he asked.

"Yes, Papa. One of the servants did it. Do you like it?"

"Very pretty," he said, inclining his head over his coffee cup to conceal his smile.

"No it ain't, it's ugly as bedamned," Lady Healy declared loudly. "But it's neat and tidy, and no one but ourselves will see it. I have had porridge made for you, Augusta."

"Thank you," Grace replied, with a longing look at the gammon and eggs the adults were consuming.

"Gussie has the same breakfast as myself," Whewett said. "There is no need to put the servants to the extra work of making gruel."

Lady Healy shook her head at such folly. "Grease has destroyed more young ladies' complexions than you would credit. It causes spots and those ugly black pores. It does well enough for mature systems. They can handle anything, but you will have Gussie blossoming into spots if you feed her lard."

Whewett cast a brief glance across the table at the petal-like complexion of Miss Farnsworth. "We certainly wouldn't want that. Eat your gruel, Gussie."

46

"It's lumpy," Grace said, putting her spoon into the unappetizing mess in her bowl. The spoon stood up straight.

"Rubbish! No one can make oat porridge like the Scots. My own cook prepared it specially for you. Now eat it up," Grandma ordered. As Grace was extremely hungry, she ate it, while the tantalizing aroma of toast, meat, and coffee hung over the table. It was the coffee that nearly undid her.

Lady Healy ruled the conversation, telling Whewett where to ride, what to check—the state of the fields for water, fences, crops. "You can take lunch at the inn you will come to a mile beyond the west pasture. No need to come all the way back here. Augusta and I can amuse ourselves. We take dinner at six. Be sure you are home in time to change."

"Yes, Grandmama," he said, in the same submissive tone as his "daughter."

When breakfast was over, Lady Healy announced, "You will go to the stable with your papa, Augusta, to see him off. Then come back. I want to test you on the Bible. I wrote you a dozen times to study your Bible."

"Yes, Grandmama."

The two escaped to the stable, oblivious of the sun shining on verdant fields and the hint of a breeze stirring the leaves above. "Sorry about the gruel," Whewett said.

"It was the coffee I regretted more. It smelled so good."

"It was bitter. The Scots may make a good lumpy batch of gruel, but they have no talent with coffee. How are you on the Bible, Doll?"

"Not terribly well versed. Is Doll a dab at it?"

47

"Nope. Try if you can beguile her with other things. You ride—get her into stories of her riding days. She's as proud as a queen of her prowess in the field." Entering the stable, he said, "Now, let us see what John had in the way of horseflesh."

The stalls were mostly empty, save for his own carriage horses. John Brougham had not been much younger than his sister. What he rode on those rare occasions when he rode at all was an ancient nag that should have been sent to the pound years ago. "Good God! Is that what I am expected to make my rounds on? I shall be a week completing the circuit."

Grace laughed to see the elegant Lord Whewett throw his leg over such a jade. "You would do better to go on foot."

"Let us hope the inn has something for hire. Well, I'm off, Augusta. Run along, and be nice to Grandma."

"Yes, Papa." She made a curtsy for the benefit of the few stableboys who gaped with interest at the visitors.

Grace returned to the house at a lagging gait, dreading the ordeal before her. As Whewett had suggested, Lady Healy was easily distracted from the Bible to boast of her skill in the saddle instead. She told tales, surely exaggerated, of hunting while hardly out of pinafores, of jumping and riding and other feats of unusual prowess. From this she went on to give advice on fomenting a wounded leg, curing colic, and such other matters as might be new to a child but were as familiar as an old ballad to Miss Farnsworth.

They took lunch together, another insufficient meal, in Grace's opinion. At its conclusion, Lady

Healy announced she always took a nap in the afternoon and suggested Gussie do the same. She did not insist, however, and the time was spent much more gainfully in scouring the house for candles to lighten her room at night, books to help pass those three or four hours of confinement, and most of all, food. Cook's presence in the kitchen made household food difficult to obtain. Apples were garnered from the orchard to augment the bonbons. At four, Lady Healy returned belowstairs, bearing a brown bag.

"I have a little present for you, Augusta."

"How nice, Grandma!" Grace smiled.

The bag was opened to reveal a skipping rope with spindle handles. The toy looked old enough to be an antique. "My own skipping rope, used by me when I was a child," Grandma said, then stood waiting for gratitude.

"Thank you," Grace said, trying to hide her disappointment.

"I knew you would be bored to flinders her. I remember my youth. Take it out in the garden and play. I shan't go out; the sun gives me a headache. I'll watch from the window. I like to see the kiddies play."

"Yes, Grandmama." Grace opened the French doors into the garden, trailing the rope behind her. She dutifully skipped, with Lady Healy smiling approval, till she was exhausted from the demanding game. As soon as she stopped, Grandma tapped sharply on the glass to indicate she should continue. The gnarled hands, whirling in circles, suggested that the pace ought to be accelerated. It was impossible. Grace skipped on, panting, her throat aching from dryness. At last she spotted Whewett returning from his rounds and looking as fagged as she felt herself. He stared in consternation to see what she was being forced into. She used his arrival as an excuse to stop.

"Poor Gussie! How did you get drawn into this cruel and unusual punishment?" he asked, but there was no ignoring the laughter in his voice. His sympathy was mixed with amusement, to see Miss Farnsworth with the perspiration standing in beads on her brow while she gasped for breath.

"A present from Grandmama . . . watching to see I make good use of it . . . at the window." Her breath gave out, and she had to wait to recover it. "Whewett, I think I am having a heart attack. If I die, use my pay to see I get a decent Christian burial. My blood will be on your hands."

"My day has been as bad. No nag at the inn. I have carried Dobbin back from the west acres. How did the Bible quiz go?"

"Short," she said, still panting, "I took your advice. If you need help in managing your stables, I can tell you exactly what ration of feed you should be giving your cattle and anything else you want to know."

"Did you get a good lunch?"

"A coddled egg. And I shan't have the strength to lift a fork at dinner."

"I'll feed you."

"Good. I'll need all my energy for this strenuous work, which you foolish grownups call play. I got in some supplies for tonight's incarceration."

"So did I. I brought you a meal from the inn. My groom will smuggle it to my valet, who will smuggle it to me, who will smuggle it through the door to you."

"Who will gratefully smuggle it to my mouth. What did—"

"I'd best go in. She's peering out at us."

"I'm going with you! I'll have an apoplexy if I must skip another skip. If she tries to send me back, *protect me*, Papa. You know my frail constitution."

"How thankful I am that my Gussie is safe in Ireland." Grace looked sulky at this thoughtless statement. "That was gauche of me. Come, I'll protect you."

They entered together. Lady Healy made no move to put her favorite out for more air and exercise. She asked Whewett many questions about the estate, which he answered briefly.

"It sounds as bad as my worst fears. I shall be lucky to get thirty-five hundred for it. It should bring five thousand easily."

"It will," he assured her. "Prices are up since you were last here."

"The agent mentioned thirty-five."

"Then he quoted a sum that would allow him to sell it in a day. He must be anxious for his commission. Don't take less than five thousand. It's a warm day," he said, mopping his brow. "Is there any ale?"

"An excellent idea. We'll both have one," Lady Healy said.

"I am thirsty, too," Grace chimed in swiftly.

"Pity I hadn't thought to have Mulkins make you more lemonade, but there is plenty of milk. Milk is good for you."

The beverages were brought. Grace was handed a glass of lukewarm milk. "It's warm," she said, looking with envy at the ale. Beads of condensation had formed on the glasses, lending the ale an appetizing look.

"That's good," the hostess said. "You should always drink your milk warm. It is easier to digest. You don't want to go putting cold drinks into your stomach when you are het up. They will give you cramps."

"*You're* having a cold drink," Grace pointed out.

"We are grown-up. Once the system is developed, it can handle anything. Now drink up your milk, and stop whining."

Whewett looked as if he would like to object, but he said nothing. The milk was unappetizing, Grace feared she would actually be sick to her stomach if she drank it. She set it aside while the others drank their ale. Lady Healy soon observed her trick and commanded her to drink it up. Grace took a tiny sip.

"All of it. Finish it off," Grandma decreed. Grace drank, turning pale with the effort.

"That will be enough for her," Whewett said when she was half-finished.

"She wants physicking, that's what ails her," Lady Healy decided. "Travel always destroys the digestion. Her appetite was excellent yesterday. When a girl goes off her feed, she wants physicking. Lucky I have my blue pills with me." She pulled the bell cord and ordered Molly to get the blue pills from Mulkins.

"I don't want a physic!" Grace insisted, but was talked down.

Whewett mentally weighed the warm milk against the pill, and thought the pill the lesser of two evils, so he said nothing. When it arrived, it was seen to be only slightly smaller than a plover's egg, but it was soon being forced down Grace's throat. Grandma rattled on about Gussie's poor health.

"The child needs exercise, Alfred. She has no wind. She was gasping like a fish on land after only half an hour with the rope. I used to skip all day when I was her age and never got winded. I knew how it would be and gave her the rope to build her up. You shall have an hour a day with the rope, missie, and see if we don't get some roses in those cheeks. Don't let her mope around the house all day playing with dolls, Alfred."

"I wish I had a doll," Grace exclaimed in a fit of defiance. "I would rather have had a doll than a rope."

"Sauce! The chit has no manners. You want to take a switch to her shoulders. It is clear you never punish her as you ought. She does just as she pleases with you. My papa would have warmed my backside if I had ever spoken to rudely."

"Augusta is a little out of sorts," Whewett said, with a warning look at Grace.

"And another thing," Lady Healy ranted on, "she don't know her Bible stories as a Christian should. We shall put her on a regime. An hour with the rope, an hour with her Bible, a good nap in the afternoon, plenty of milk, and early to bed. We shall administer a stronger physic, too, if the blue pill don't work."

"Papa!" Grace said, looking to Whewett for protection. He sat on, nodding his agreement.

"Your grandmother is right, dear."

She held in all her spleen, but she looked ready to explode. If it had been for longer than one more day, she would have rebelled, but for one day more she could stand it. A hundred pounds, she repeated silently to herself. Three hundred and sixty-five days of Mrs. Bixworth. It was worth it.

"There, she is in the sulks," Lady Healy declared. "Run along to your room, missie. If you cannot control your temper, you have no business sitting with adults. Your manners are so poor, you shall eat in your room tonight."

It was not yet five o'clock. This sounded as if she was being sent there for the entire evening. She opened her mouth to object.

"Quite right, Grandma," Whewett said. "Her manners are sadly wanting. Let her stay in her room till she has had dinner. If she is good, we shall let her come down and play to us later." As soon as the speech was out, he fell to wondering if Miss Farnsworth could play.

Her reply reassured him. "May I? I was looking at the music on the pianoforte earlier and would like to try it."

"If you are good," Grandma said, then dismissed her.

As soon as she was gone, the old lady turned to Whewett with a twinkle in her rheumy old eyes. "She has bottom, the rascal. Wanted to cut up at me and at you, too. I like her excessively, Alfred. If she were not my granddaughter, I would adopt her. You have taught her a little something about stable management, I am happy to see."

For Lady Healy to admit that anyone but herself knew anything about a horse was an admission of no small magnitude. He was happy Miss Farnsworth had passed this important test. "She is fond of riding," he said.

"But she ain't a tomboy, and that is all to the

good. She is cross with me. I shall buy her a present. She wants a doll. You must do it for me, but let her know it is *my* present. Take her to the village tomorrow and get her one."

"That is not necessary," he said, wishing to avoid the village, especially in Miss Farnsworth's company.

"Do it, I say!"

"Gussie has dozens of dolls."

"She does not have one from *me*, and she hasn't got one *with* her."

"I should finish assessing Willowcrest tomorrow, Grandma. I cannot stay much longer."

"Pshaw! I never see you for years on end. Take your time about the estate. It will all be Gussie's one day. We don't want to gyp her by undervaluing it."

Whewett was so cheered to hear the estate was destined for his daughter that he agreed to stay, though he knew it would be hard on Miss Farnsworth. She was having a worse time then he had ever envisioned. A break, a trip to the village, might please her. There was no real danger in it.

When he went to his room to change for dinner, he tapped on her door and was admitted. She had been fed early and was just setting aside her tray. "I hope a full stomach puts you in a good mood," he said.

"When my stomach is full of pig's cheek and bread pudding, it is not likely to do so. The adults' dinner was not ready. I have been fed the servants' meal. Even at Bixworths' I never had to eat bread pudding."

"It won't be for much longer. Only a few days," he said placatingly.

"A few days! Surely we leave *tomorrow*! You said two days when we began."

"I'm dashed sorry, Miss Farnsworth. Something's come up."

A worried frown flew to her brow. "Have I ruined everything? Oh, I am sorry, but to have to drink warm milk, nearly sour, and that enormous blue pill!"

"I am the one who should apologize. I am really damnably sorry. You haven't ruined anything. Quite the contrary. She likes a show of spirits. Actually . . ." He blushed to mention giving a doll to a grown woman and said vaguely, "There are a few estate matters to tend to, but the whole is to go to Augusta, and I cannot be too abrupt with her."

"Is it indeed? I am happy for you. Not so happy with the regime she is setting up for me, but—"

"It won't be so bad. We are to be allowed into the village tomorrow afternoon. We'll make a long stay of it to give you a respite. We must be cautious, but no one there knows us, so there can be no harm."

"It sounds wonderful."

"I know you're having a devil of a time. I didn't think it would be this bad, but really, you are doing a marvelous job. A professional actress couldn't do half so well. She was mighty impressed with your knowledge of stable management. And I was a fool to ask you to play for us before learning whether you could."

"Lord Whewett, *all* ladies play the pianoforte. Badly, most of us, but we must have the rudiments, you know, or we may not call ourselves ladies. Perhaps you don't think I really am a lady?" she asked, and scrutinized him closely.

"You were at pains to make me believe you were

a child," he answered, which told her nothing. "I must wash and change. Lord, I'm bushed. There is nothing so tiring as dragging along on a glue pot."

"Try skipping for an hour in the sun."

"The early nights won't be so hard to take after all." He went to the door, waggled his fingers, and left.

Grace sat on, thinking. He hadn't answered her question. *Did* Whewett think that, at bottom, she was nothing more than an adventuress? She had capitulated too easily to his bizarre request to play his daughter. And what did it matter what he thought of her anyway? He would pay her salary; of that she had no doubts. But still she wished he would not think ill of her after the charade was over.

Chapter Five

It was after seven before Grace was called to the saloon, by which time she had already eaten an apple and three bonbons and was curious to discover what food Whewett had brought her from the inn. As soon as she entered the room, she was ordered to the pianoforte, where she acquitted herself as well as could be expected on an instrument that had not been tuned for fifteen years. She had a pretty voice, not outstandingly beautiful, but more than acceptable to a slightly deaf grandmother and a very grateful widower.

"You play well, Augusta. There will be something else to add to your regime," Lady Healy told her. "You shall have an hour a day to cure you of that habit you have picked up of racing ahead with the right hand. I believe you left out some sharps and flats, too, for some of the notes sounded very odd, but it was a genteel performance. A lady ought not to play too well."

This addition to the regime was welcome, and Grace smiled her satisfaction. Whewett pointed out that the piano's being out of tune was to blame for the sour notes, which incited the dame to inform him the piano could not be held to blame for the wrong notes *sung*.

Their little altercation was interrupted by a caller at the door, which caused Grace to suffer a tremble. It was only the estate agent, Bronfman, come to tell them he had a party interested in looking at Willowcrest. "Daugherty is the name, from Kent. They have been on the lookout for something in the neighborhood, so I called them. They can be here in four days, if that suits you, milady?"

"Excellent, it allows time to have the girls give the place a good scouring," Lady Healy agreed.

"I cannot stay that long," Whewett mentioned, but saw no reason why his presence should be necessary.

The hour for inspection was set, three o'clock in the afternoon; then Bronfman left. Lady Healy discussed what must be done to the house. "Some girls hired from the village to wax and polish, to smarten us up." When Whewett politely declined the furnishings of the house, she decided to sell the place furnished.

This settled, she next turned to Augusta, to begin a series of impertinent questions regarding her studies. "Do you know how to add, subtract, multiply?" When told that Augusta was an accomplished mathematician, she fired off numbers that a lady of two and twenty had no difficulty in answering. An old French text was discovered on a shelf and pushed into Grace's hands for her to translate. This also was successful.

"She ain't a complete ignoramus, I am happy to see. This Invers must be a decent creature."

All too soon it was eighty-thirty. Already Lady Healy had glanced thrice at the long-case clock in the corner. Her third look made clear the clock had stopped, but she was too proud to admit her sight was failing. "Time for bed, Augusta. Don't forget the teeth and your prayers. Body and soul, you see. Come and kiss me good-night before you go." Grace kissed the aged cheek. "Your papa, too," she was reminded.

As she advanced to Whewett, she noticed he was wearing that smile she was coming to know well, half laughing at her, half pitying her predicament, and half-admiring of her performance. When she leaned toward him, he kissed her just at the corner of her lips. "Good night, Doll," he said. There was no roughness of a day's growth of beard. Had he shaved before dinner? How odd. He hadn't bothered last night.

When Grace went to her room, she wondered if Whewett planned to sneak out after Grandma retired. Was that why he had shaved? Had he met some lightskirt in the village while he was at the inn? He didn't seem that sort of gentleman, but then he was a widower and away from home. Perhaps she'd tease him about it.

In the Purple Saloon Lady Healy smiled her satisfaction. "She is a lovely lass, Alfred."

"Yes, I am proud of her."

"I have been thinking, as those Kent people are coming so soon to see the place, you might as well stay."

"It is not at all convenient for me. I told you so when Bronfman mentioned four days."

"It would be in every way better if you would ride about the place with Daugherty. Must be Irish, eh, with a name like that? Bronfman will try to take advantage of me. He'll point out the worst features."

"He'll hardly do that. He's trying to sell."

"What I mean is, Daugherty will mention them, and Bronfman will make it an excuse to lower my price. I need a man to protect my interests. It may make a thousand difference in the price."

Whewett frowned. "I have things I should be doing at home."

"Surely your daughter's welfare is of equal importance!" she pointed out curtly.

"Of course, but—"

"You'll stay, then."

"Yes, Grandmama. I'll drop my man of business a note tonight."

"Good. Now we must discuss the Scotland properties. I have promised five thousand to the Hunt Club there. My Willie started it up, you know. It is to be endowed in his name. The balance of what I possess is for Gussie. I mean to remain in Scotland till I die. It is my home. Once I am gone, however, you will want to dispose of the property and get the money. It is the sensible course. Bruce MacKinnon, a neighbor, has dropped hints he is interested. Don't give it away. It is worth ten thousand."

"Yes, I'll arrange it. Gussie would have no use for a Scottish property."

This innocent remark caused his companion to turn querulous. "It seems not, as she was never

61

once allowed to visit Scotland in twelve years. She should have come at least once. She ain't sickly, and she ain't shy. Why did you keep her from me?"

"I couldn't send her alone, and you know I am busy."

"You could have sent her with Invers. I have an excellent opinion of Invers. She has trained Gussie well."

Of course he could not tell the truth, but he must say something. "Gussie is pretty young yet."

"*I* ain't! If she is ever to come, it must be soon."

"Yes," he said, to have done with the subject.

"Good. I am glad you agree with me. I shall have Mulkins prepare my posset and bring it to my room. I am for the tick, Alfred. I ain't much company for you, I fear. Help me out of this demmed chair. The chairs are all too low in this house."

He hauled her up, called Mulkins, then helped her upstairs. Within minutes, he was tapping at Grace's door. Her room was cheerier with more candles to relieve the heavy shadows. She was happier, too, with a copy of Richardson's *Pamela* open before her.

"Brushing up on the Bible, are you?" he asked, glancing at the book.

"I am more agreeably entertained, reading up on the rewards of virtue."

He lifted the tome to see the title. "Pretty warm stuff for my twelve-year-old daughter," he quizzed.

"Buy her a copy. One is never too young to learn about the wickedness of men. I consider the book *de riqueur* for servants like myself, and I like Pamela, the heroine. A pity Mrs. Bixworth had no wastrel son to fall in love with me. Even the initial would have matched Pamela's Mr. B."

Whewett lifted a satirical brow. "A great pity. It would have enlivened your dull days no end to have the pleasure of being pursued by a rake."

"My days did not lack liveliness, I promise you. When I was not pulling Dora out from under a horse's hooves, I was rescuing Ellie Lou from the briny deep."

"It puts skipping and Bible reading quite in the shade, eh, Doll?"

"You should not call me that in front of Grandma. She likes to hear her own name being used on a younger person. She resents her age so."

"It must be the devil when they start building the chairs so low you can't get out of them un-aided."

Grace adopted a confidential tone. "Did you know her hair is dyed? I caught Mulkins with the dye pot going to her room when I came upstairs."

"And she letting on it was a posset! It's sweet, though, to have held on to her vanity for so long. I seemed to turn old at thirty or so."

Grace looked at his smooth cheek and discerned a fresh dose of cologne emanating from him. "I don't think you are quite free of vanity yet, sir. A man does not shave twice in one day if he does not care for his appearance. I think you are on the scent of some female, Whewett."

She watched in astonishment as a pink flush ascended from his collar. What had possessed him to have a fresh shave, only to come in here and be mocked by this bright-eyed young lady?

"It's true!" she charged, and laughed loudly. "Now *do* tell me all about her. You must have met her at the inn, unless she was lurking about the west acres."

At least she didn't suspect she was the cause. The pink faded, leaving only an air of consciousness. "I always shave twice a day," he said with a fair semblance of ease.

"You didn't yesterday. Your cheek was rough last night. You'll have to slip out quietly, Whewett. Grandma wouldn't like it."

"I'm not slipping out!" he exclaimed. "You make me sound like a libertine."

She gave him a saucy smile. "No, you are making yourself sound like one. A gentleman might take a glass of wine with a lady in the evening without being a libertine. Now, before you shock me with any further lechery, let us speak of more important things. I mean, of course, food."

Whewett was remarkably glad to change the subject. "I thought it would not be long before we came back to that. I daresay you haven't had a bite in half an hour, except for a peck of apples and box of bonbons."

"It's been more than half an hour since *I* ate," she reminded him, as he went to his room for the food. He returned with a roasted chicken in oiled paper and an apple tart.

"A whole meal!" she gurgled. "How splendid. And how messy. I cannot eat an apple tart with my fingers. And what do I do with a chicken carcass after I have devoured the rest?"

"I thought you would eat the bones, too, like a whale."

"Whales are not carnivores, Whewett," she said, daintily dismembering a leg and nibbling on it. "I'll wrap the bones up for you to throw away when you are riding tomorrow. Would you like some of this?"

"It looks good," he said, accepting the other leg. "A pity we have no wine for our picnic."

"So much more appetizing than sour milk, my youthful innards notwithstanding. Did Grandma say anything interesting after I left?"

"It is settled you are to be her sole heir but for the Hunt Club in Scotland. Mulkins and the servants will get some bequests, of course, though she didn't say so."

"I am happy for Augusta, but I feel badly about fooling Lady Healy."

"I don't. She might have left it all to the Scottish hunters if you hadn't come. She is miffed with me for not having sent Gussie to her, but this visit convinces me they would not have rubbed along at all. She is shy, my Gussie."

"Tell me about her," Grace said.

"It's hard for me to be objective. I love her, you see. She is quiet," he began, with a fond smile. "She's been too much alone, with no mother, you know. We are close, but it's not the same. She often rides out with me on my rounds when she is not at her lessons. She's bright, plays the pianoforte, speaks French, but not so fluently as you. Neither does she do so well in her sums."

"As to the sums, there is no teacher like necessity. Besides, you forget I'm old enough to be teaching Augusta."

"That's true. She's a good rider. I made her be. She was frightened at first."

"What of her friends—the girl with the toothache?"

"There are no youngsters living close by. The one with the toothache, Sally Grimsby, was just visiting six months ago. Gussie makes a big thing of anyone who happens along. A cousin or whatnot in the house for a few days takes on great importance."

"I expect she has an active imagination. Those . . . lonesome children do."

"Too much so. I had a librarian cataloging my books a while ago, and Gussie took to pretending his daughter was her sister. For two weeks she was happy as a lark and talked on for ages about her sister. I worry a little about her. I should send her to a seminary, I expect, but I'm too selfish."

"That's not really selfishness. I imagine you're a very nice sort of father. Kind, caring, easy to wind round a thumb," she added with a pert look. "Is Gussie a winder?"

"Not at all."

"You wouldn't recognize it if she were."

"Perhaps you're right. She talked me into letting her go to Ireland with Mary. I hope she isn't homesick—she's been gone a month. They'll be back soon."

"Perhaps she'll be there waiting for you when you return."

"Not quite that soon. In any case, my sister is bringing her back, so Gussie would not be alone at Downsfield." He glanced at the remains of chicken. "What are we to do with the rest of this meat?"

"Eat it, of course. Do you have a pocket knife to carve that lovely breast?"

Whewett shook his head, wondering where such a small girl put so much food. He cut it into thin strips, to be eaten with the fingers. "Does your sister know you are here?" Grace asked.

"I didn't write. They know at home where I am, and would tell her if she came."

"I hope she doesn't come landing in with the real Augusta!"

"Not much chance of that. But enough of my problems. What will you do when you leave?"

"I'll try to find Miss Thomas, get a new position. My hundred pounds gives me time to look around."

Whewett mentally compared their futures. "It sounds a hard life for a young girl. Yes, I know you are all of two and twenty, but that happens to sound young to me. Would you like to go to Ireland? I could speak to Mary about you. With two girls, she might have some use for you."

"I never thought of Ireland," Grace said pensively. If Mary were like her brother, she would be a congenial employer.

"Think about it. It is unfair that one of my daughters get so much, while the other is thrown into the cruel world with a measly hundred pounds."

"All things are relative. A measly hundred pounds sounds a princely sum to me at the moment."

Whewett soon left but continued thinking of what they had discussed. It did indeed seem hard that poor Miss Farnsworth be put to such shifts to earn her bread. She had been reared a lady and was not equipped for this hard life that was thrust upon her. Such a girl might come to grief—a lecherous son or husband, for instance, in some home where she was working, could ruin her.

Behind the closed door Grace entertained no such lugubrious thoughts. She ate her chicken, carefully wrapped the apple tart up for the morrow, read her book, and occasionally thought of her good fortune at soon having a hundred pounds in her reticule.

Chapter Six

Lady Healy blamed her headache the next morning on the weather. The air was not so cool and clear as the air of the Highlands. Her headache, however, was no reason for Augusta's regime to be interrupted. Grace was sent off to the garden with her rope before the sun became too warm. Whewett was back on his glue pot to decide which corners of the estate were to be concealed from Daugherty and which brought to his attention. With Bronfman's help, local girls were hired to clean up the house. They were busy with goose wing to dust the library books, with beeswax and turpentine to restore the gleam to old wood, with soap and water to clean windows, and with damp tea leaves to keep down the dust when they swept the carpets.

Grace skipped for the ten minutes Lady Healy observed her, then darted off to walk through the grounds and enjoy herself. When Whewett returned for lunch, Lady Healy felt well enough to come to the table, but she was feeling peaky.

"I'll have a lie-down this afternoon while you take Augusta into Wickfield," she decided. The old lady was so unlike herself that Grace got a piece of plum cake onto her plate without censure.

The day was pleasant, with just a hint of early autumn approaching. Whewett let down the carriage windows. "You have a rare treat in store for you today, Doll," he said.

"Indeed I have. I can lower my voice from a childish squeak and not call you Papa."

"Even better, you are about to receive a present that will help pass those dull hours in your room. Grandma has ordered me to buy you a doll, to make up for being harsh about the blue pill."

He thought she would laugh and was surprised by her wistful smile. "How touching. I feel a perfect wretch. I didn't even take the pill, but held it under my tongue till I could hide it in my handkerchief."

"Here I have been pitying you for nought. But still, your duplicity is to be rewarded with a new doll."

"Must we?"

"Gussie will love it."

"Lucky Gussie! *She* enjoys the pleasures of Ireland, and gets *my* reward." Grace spoke without thinking and was surprised to see Whewett took her seriously.

"That is true. You must have a present as well."

"I was joking, Whewett. Does your daughter still play with dolls?"

"Not in public, but when I go to tuck her in at
70

night, she is surrounded by half a dozen of them. Sisters all."

"Then we shall pick out one for her, and you take it home."

"A little difficulty has just occurred to me. . . ."

"What a mountain of imagination! One whole difficulty."

"One specific thing I hadn't thought of before. Gussie's future correspondence with her grandmother will discuss this visit, or ought to. I must dream up some explanation for Gussie."

"That's true," Grace said, frowning. "You must edit her letters carefully, to see she doesn't give the show away."

"The future holds a few problems, but the visit is going marvelously well."

"Best of all, it's nearly over."

Whewett jabbed at his collar, looking as guilty as sin. "I—I have a confession, Miss Farnsworth."

She turned a wrathful brown eye on him. "Whewett, don't—pray do *not* tell me the show has been held over."

"Just a few more days. I'm dreadfully sorry."

"I'll *never* get away from here! Root will sprout from my feet. I'll grow old and wrinkled while still in short skirts."

"The thing is, you see, Daugherty isn't coming till Friday, and she wants me to show him around."

"Let Bronfman show him around. That's what he's being paid for. The Daughertys aren't coming till three, and that means we shan't get away till Saturday."

"Just three more days," he said hopefully.

"It's too long. You said two days altogether. That's all I agreed to."

"I'll pay you more—anything you ask," he said in desperation.

"It's not the money. It's just—just too long. I'm not used to such wicked deceit. I can't relax a moment."

"You can relax now, when we are alone, I mean."

"Relax? With my skirts hiked halfway up my legs and my hair pinned into these bows, and going to buy a doll? You have a strange idea of how I relax." Grace felt close to tears from sheer vexation.

"I'm sorry, Miss Farnsworth. Truly I am. I didn't intend to impose on you so brutally. Please bear with me. I'll make it up to you. Five hundred pounds."

"Don't be absurd. I can't take such a sum from you. It would be—immoral. I *am* immoral. I didn't mind so much before I knew Lady Healy. Oh, and she is so nice, buying me a present, when I didn't even take the pill. Could you not make some excuse to leave earlier, Whewett?"

He damped down his frustration and answered civilly. "I can, if you insist, but she's right about the sale. Bronfman will sell her out cheap to close the deal and get his commission. She wants me to keep an eye on things. It is only common sense, and common courtesy, too, when you consider it is all to be my daughter's one day. I understand, of course, that my family's welfare is not your first concern. No reason it should be."

Grace acknowledged that from his point of view, staying was the sane course. She gave a weary sigh and said, "I have nothing special to do the next few days except find Miss Thomas."

"Perhaps we could do that today," he suggested eagerly.

"Her neighbor said she had let her house. The new occupants might know her address. Will you take me to them?"

"Gladly. Shall I make inquiries for you? They might think it odd, your going alone."

"Everyone always thinks it odd, but I'm pretty good at making excuses."

Whewett's relief at her capitulation was tinged with guilt. He was treating Miss Farnsworth abominably and decided to assuage his grief by buying her a grand present. It was only fair. Her gift from Grandma was going to Gussie. He owed her for that as well as the rest. One hundred pounds didn't begin to cover it. He would make her take the five hundred.

They set about the business of buying the doll first. Grace began looking at simple rag dolls, of the sort she had had as a child. Whewett said, "Grandma gave me a whole guinea to spend. We can get one with a dish head, if you like."

"Good gracious! We're rich. We can buy a whole family. Would Gussie like one with a dish head?"

"She has all kinds. I believe Grandma's plan is to outdo the others."

"That sounds like her. Oh, look, Whew—Papa," she said, as the clerk came up to them. "See the pretty one with blond curls. I always wanted blond curls and blue eyes myself. Let us get that one."

"The little lady has excellent taste," the clerk said, and handed it down to her.

Grace admired the fine workmanship; the doll's eyelids were hinged to open and shut mechanically, and even had eyelashes stuck into them. The gown was an elegant silk, with pink ribbons. It was a real work of art. "Isn't it beautiful!" she exclaimed.

"Is that the one you want?" Whewett asked.

"Yes, please."

It was purchased, using up Lady Healy's whole guinea. "Sure you're really over twenty?" he asked quietly as they walked out. "You looked very pleased with your toy."

"Some toys are works of art. I hope Doll appreciates it."

"Gussie, you mean."

"You call her Doll sometimes, don't you?"

Whewett wondered why a simple lie to confirm this should stick in his throat, when his whole life had become a lie. Perhaps it was because it involved his daughter, whom he had never in his life called Doll.

"Don't you?" Grace repeated, wondering at his uneasy manner.

"I call her lots of things. Now that we have her present, I want to buy something for my other daughter."

"This daughter doesn't take presents from gentlemen, thank you all the same."

"Oh, come now, surely I may replace Grandma's gift, which Gussie has stolen from you, without infringing on the proprieties. I think a piece of jewelry would be suitable," he said tentatively.

It was, of all gifts, the most inappropriate. Gentlemen gave jewelry to their mistresses. Did he think that because she had agreed to this charade, she was no better than she should be? "Think again," she said firmly.

"I didn't mean a diamond necklace or tiara, so you need not fly into a pelter. Some token of my gratitude for your excellent performance. A watch—"

"I prefer cash. The sum has been agreed upon," she said cooly.

"Even the pious Pamela let her virtue be rewarded," he mentioned. When she looked away, he realized it was time to change the subject. "Did you finish the book?"

"No, it is in three volumes. At the rate our performance is dragging on, I shall finish all three before we leave. Actually Pamela hasn't got much reward yet for her travails. But I believe she is talking Mr. B. into marrying her."

"He does."

"Whewett! How dare you spoil the ending for me! What a cruel stunt. Now I shan't have any interest to read the rest."

"That's just the beginning. Things don't heat up till she makes the mistake of marrying the bounder. You servant girls must be very careful whom you take up with, or even marry."

"I'll worry about that if the time ever comes."

"You really should not have accepted this job with me, you know. It was rash and foolish of you."

"I'm perfectly aware of it. I hadn't much choice. I had three pennies in my pocket after paying for my tea, and nowhere to go."

Whewett shook his head in rueful wonder. "Did you really have no more money than that?"

"I would not have been cheating the coaching company if I had the full fare. I am not a criminal, you know, and I don't accept jewelry from gentlemen, either." As soon as the words were out, she wished she could unsay them. His look of blank shock told her how far off the mark she was, to suspect any ulterior motive in the offer. When her meaning sank in, Whewett looked confused and rather embarrassed. It seemed best to drop the matter.

She glanced across the street and said, "There is a park with a pond and geese. Shall we go and see them?" Grace led off, and he followed with a frown on his brow.

She went to the pond's edge and knelt to coax a goose to her with very little success. Whewett did not join her. The feeling of embarrassment ebbed as she played with the fowl. One fat white goose reminded her of Esmeralda, her own favorite goose at home, and she tried to lure it to her. She snapped her fingers, and finally leaned out to try to reach it. There were some elderly folks sitting on benches nearby.

"Pretty girl," an old man said to Whewett. "Your daughter?"

"Yes."

"Best grab her before she falls in," the man suggested, with a shake of his head at the folly of children.

Whewett went to the pond to retrieve the wayward daughter. "You worry me considerably," he said. "I suffer a recurring delusion that you are indeed twelve years old, and I have abducted a child from her parents."

"You didn't abduct me. I joined you voluntarily."

His dark eyes studied her. "That worries me even more."

She felt uneasy, having her common sense judged by this man, and quickly changed the subject. "I like geese," she said vaguely. "They're so pretty in water, and the goslings are just at that awkward stage when they don't know whether they are still goslings, or all grown-up."

"One tells by the feathers, amongst other things," he said, scanning her own childish garments. But when his eyes lifted to her face, he wondered how he had ever mistaken Grace for a child. There was maturity in those eyes, and a certain precision of features that young girls lacked. A feeling of strangeness was growing between them as they stood together. "Would you like an ice?" he asked, to break the tension.

"Yes, it's warm. I haven't had an ice in ages."

"Do you not have ices when you take your charges to that ocean Ellie Lou likes to fall into? There are stands set up on the beach at home."

"The girls do. A governess must maintain her dignity."

He shook his head. "And you hungrier than the two of them put together, if I know anything. You really do worry me, Doll."

They had two ices at a parlor, then went into the street again. Whewett felt a tugging at his sleeve. As he turned, Grace darted off to look into a shop window. "It's Mr. Whewett, isn't it?" a loud voice called. Turning, he saw the woman from the stage, whose name he could not remember and whose protruding eyes he could not forget.

"How is Lady Healy?" the woman demanded, with all the familiarity of an old acquaintance.

"Very well, thank you."

"Are you having any luck selling Willowcrest?"

77

"A man from Kent is coming to look at it this week."

"That's fast work. Still, there'll be many a looker before there's a taker." She folded her arms, planted her feet comfortably apart, obviously settling in for a lengthy chat. She glanced around and discovered Grace behind them. "Why, there is Miss Jones! Quite a coincidence, all three of us meeting. I'll just go and see if she got to her governess all right, for she wasn't met at the coaching stop. She ran off down the street all alone, poor tyke. Unconscionable the way some girls are let run wild. She wouldn't of heard yet if she got the brother she wanted, I expect."

Whewett was left to ponder this last mystery, till a memory stirred of Miss Farnsworth's story on the stage. He walked along to the next shop and stood looking in the window till Mrs. Sempleton had had her chat with Miss Jones and was on her way. Grace waited till the woman had turned a corner before looking for Whewett.

"Very nearly caught out!" she exclaimed. "Wouldn't you know, we would meet the one person who knows I am not Augusta."

"That woman had the memory of an elephant. She even remembered your mama is in the throes of childbirth."

"She remembered I wanted a brother, too." Grace laughed.

"You will be happy to hear I have got one, just yesterday. Mama is calling him Alfred, after my own papa."

"Let us get out of here before she returns. We'll go to Miss Thomas's cottage now."

An inquiry was of no help. The lady of the house

78

was out, and the servants knew nothing. The afternoon was fast drawing to a close, and it was time to return to Willowcrest.

Chapter Seven

Lady Healy had arisen from her nap when they returned to Willowcrest. Grace was allowed to sit with the grown-ups and have a glass of lemonade. "How did you like your new doll, eh?" was the first word said. "Did you pick out a pretty one?"

"A beautiful one, Grandma. Thank you so much. She has blond curls, blue eyes, and the loveliest gown." Grace tore off the paper with a fine show of childish enthusiasm.

Grandma clucked over it with as much pleasure as the recipient. When Grace went to sit down, she picked up the doll to take with her, to please the old lady.

"It is nice to see the young ones in no hurry to grow up," Lady Healy said aside to Whewett. "All too soon Gussie will be wearing long skirts. What a quiz she will look, not five feet high. I am closer to six. She'll be having beaus, first thing you know.

Are there any good *partis* for her around Downs-field?"

"We haven't begun to think of that yet."

"*You* haven't. Let us hear Augusta speak for herself." She raised her voice. "Have you got a sweetheart, Gussie?"

"Not yet, Grandmama, but I am looking about me."

"I wager you are. She's half grown up on you, Alfred. Best face the fact you'll soon be losing her. It don't do for a father to depend too much on his daughter, or vice versa. You'll up and die on her and leave her a spinster. We don't want Gussie sinking into a spinster."

"I shan't, Grandma. I do not depend entirely on Papa," Grace said, with a saucy look at Whewett.

"Ha, she has an eye on some lad already. She'll never say so before you. I'll get her alone one of these days and discover the whole. How about yourself, Alfred? Do you never think of marrying again? Irene's been dead a decade. You need a son and heir for Downsfield."

"There is no hurry. Gussie and I rub along fine."

"You and Gussie do, but when Lady Augusta makes her bows, it will be a different story. She must go up to London for her debut. A growing gel needs a mother to teach her the ropes. Even before that time, there are things Gussie must learn about her body and feelings. A man ain't the one to tell her."

Whewett looked uncomfortable as he sipped his wine. Lady Healy continued her counsel "It is all well and good to have a proper regard for Irene, but sentiment can be carried too far. I wager you would

81

have taken a wife before now if you didn't have a loose widow or light-o'-love nearby to amuse you."

"I would prefer not to discuss it at this time," he said curtly, with a quick look at Grace.

"Your daughter ain't a Bath miss, I hope. There is nothing worse than a missish gel who blushes at the simple facts of life. Has your papa got a mistress, Gussie? Tell me the truth."

Grace was happy that someone other than herself was the butt of the old dame's intrusive questions. "I don't know, Grandmama," she replied.

"It wouldn't surprise me a bit. Better a wife than a convenience. Perhaps Gussie has someone picked out for you, a nice mama for herself. She writes me letters, you must know. Oh, yes, I know things." She nodded smugly at this and cast a conspiratorial wink at Grace.

Whewett blinked in astonishment. "What nonsense have you been writing, Augusta?" he demanded sternly.

"Now we have him on the anxious seat," Lady Healy crowed. "He has been found out."

Mischief danced in Grace's eyes as she said, "I'm sorry, Papa. Was I not supposed to tell about your lady friend?"

"She told me," Grandma cackled. "I do not disapprove, Alfred, so long as she is a proper lady. I was married twice myself. Well now, I am feeling better after my nap. I shall go and harry those lazy girls I hired into doing a decent job. Don't go upstairs, Augusta. I shall be back presently. Haul me up, Alfred."

As soon as they were alone, Grace turned a brightly curious eye on Whewett. "You had best inform me about this mysterious lady you've been making up to behind my back."

"I haven't a notion what she was talking about."

"Whewett, don't be missish. You are plenty old enough to have a *chère amie*, if it is the woman's ineligibility that restrains you."

"I do not have a *chère amie!*"

"I am happy to hear it. As I am about to be severely quizzed about your friend, you must tell me at least her name, and a few rough facts about her background. Is she a widow, spinster, what?"

"Invent anyone you like to satisfy her. There is no such person. And I'll tell you something else, miss! I am not flattered you think I would be looking out for an old widow or spinster for a wife."

"I did not say *old*. You are a widower yourself, so you cannot take exception to that. I shouldn't think a gentleman of your years would be dangling after a deb."

Her every word incensed him more deeply. "Gentlemen of *any* age, Miss Farnsworth, prefer pretty young girls to aging spinsters. I am not quite a doddering old fool yet."

"Good gracious, I have wounded your vanity. I am excessively sorry, Whewett. I shall make it up to you."

"How do you propose to do that?"

"I shall invent, for your delight, a lady of unparalleled beauty. She shall have youth, fortune, accomplishment, pedigree. In short, a princess out of a fairy tale."

He listened, amused. "Much good an *imaginary* lady will do me. Be sure you give her a sense of humor."

Grace tossed him an arch smile. "She shall certainly require that. Fear not, all virtues shall be hers. Would you like her a trifle on the blue side, just a twilight tinge? And vivacious into the bargain?"

"I see what you are up to, making the lady the complement to myself. You are conferring on *her* all those elements lacking in myself. I am half in love with her already."

"Only half? You are hard to please, sir. What shall we call this paragon?"

"What else but Pamela?"

"Are you quite sure? She may go off into swoons every time you get near her and want her virtue rewarded, too. Let us call her—"

The shuffling tread of Lady Healy brought their discussion to a halt. "They are a lazy enough lot, the village girls," she scolded, "but they have good strong backs. Now, where were we?"

"We were discussing Papa's girlfriend," Grace answered helpfully.

"So we were. He will contradict every word you utter, so we shall send him off to his room."

"There is a change!" Grace smiled.

"Run along, Alfred. Your secrets are all going to come out now."

"If Gussie breathes a word of my women, I shall box her ears soundly. And so I warn you, miss," he added with a menacing look at Grace.

"You never lay a hand on her. That's why she is such a saucy minx." Lady Healy laughed merrily, for she liked to see anyone discomposed. "Now, tell me all about Mrs. Elton," she said eagerly as Whewett strolled out the door.

The name was a boon to Grace. It supplied some notion of the woman's status: a widow, obviously.

Her companion nudged her on with more clues. "What was she doing at Downsfield for a week? You said Alfred was mighty taken with her."

Grace began to fabricate a tale. "She came to visit us."

"Something to do with your clothing, wasn't it?"

"Yes, that is why she came."

"But she cannot be only a modiste."

"Oh, no." Grace proceeded to make Mrs. Elton a family connection on Whewett's side, the widow of a cousin. She was a blond enchantress, whose hand was sought by all men.

"She sounds a proper hussy to me," the grandmother said at the end of the tale. "Blond curls and silken gowns don't make a good mother. Is she nice to *you*, Augusta? That is what is important."

Grace realized she had allowed herself to be carried away. "She seemed very nice," she said uncertainly.

"Ho, they're all nice till they catch their prey. I don't care for the sound of her. She is only after the title. I shall tell Whewett so. He don't want a proud beauty who will be trailing him off to London for the season, abandoning you. He wants a more settled sort of lady."

She continued with these animadversions for some time. Grace feared she had inadvertently made future trouble for Whewett, if he did indeed plan to marry this Mrs. Elton. She tried to tame down her description, but her first extravagant outpouring had made a vivid impression, and Lady Healy took the lady in violent dislike, sight unseen.

When it was time to eat, Grace was told she would eat in the nursery. "For I must speak to your papa about this Elton creature." Grandma scowled. "Ask him to step down, Gussie."

Grace went upstairs and tapped at Whewett's bedroom door. His valet was just brushing the shoulders of his evening jacket. "You can leave us, Jenner," Whewett said. "Come in, Gussie. What's up? You look worried."

"I have made a *dreadful* mistake, and I'm very sorry."

"She hasn't found out?" he asked in alarm.

"That I am not Augusta? No, but I have landed you in a pickle. I hope your heart is not *quite* set on Mrs. Elton?"

He looked bewildered. "Who the devil is Mrs. Elton?"

"The lady who visited you at Downsfield, and you fell in love with. You cannot have forgotten her in six months!"

"I don't know what you're talking about."

"Think! She was helping Gussie with her clothing. I assume she must be a close friend or family connection. I said she was your cousin's widow."

Whewett touched his forehead. "Oh, Mrs. Elton. I remember her now."

"Well, who is she?"

He threw up his hand and laughed. "A dressmaker from the village. A schoolteacher's widow. She was out some time ago to make up clothes for Augusta's trip to Ireland. I recall my daughter had one of her infatuations with the woman. As Mrs. Elton was genteel, she took dinner with us and Invers. Gussie was fond of her. That is the sum and total of the great romance."

"What a take-in." Grace looked unconvinced.

"Gussie's letter hinted it was you who were fond of her."

"No, she is an older woman. She must be forty."

"That is not so old. You must have had an eye for her. Augusta would not have made it up out of whole cloth."

"Yes, she would," he said baldly. "She probably hoped I would marry the woman and give her a mother. She was a nice little old lady."

"Oh, dear, and I told Grandma she was beautiful—gave her a sense of humor, liveliness, and all, just as you ordered. She has taken the idea Mrs. Elton is only after your title. She is convinced Augusta will be abandoned while the pair of you flaunt your bodies in London."

"She must take me for a prime simpleton!"

"No, Mrs. Elton for a prime hussy. You are guilty of no more than a susceptibility to incomparables, as you told me yourself all men are."

Whewett looked at her in the mirror as he adjusted his cravat. "If you were my daughter, I'd turn you over my knee for such impertinence as criticizing your elders."

"You're ruining that nice design your valet made," she said, unfazed. "I wager you've never laid a hand on Doll. I have just been thinking these past days what a lovely father you would make."

Whewett's eyes flashed dangerously, and he gave the tie a yank that ruined it entirely. "Very flattering. And was that the great trouble, that I cannot marry old Mrs. Elton?"

"At the moment your cravat is the problem. Lean down. I am a bit of a dab with cravats. I used to help Papa." He hesitated a moment before turning from the mirror. "You had best sit down, Whewett. You're too tall."

"I bend like a reed to your ministrations," he said, and bent but did not sit, as he wanted to see the tie in the mirror.

Grace arranged the cravat, chatting nonchalantly all the while, unaware that Whewett was engrossed with their image in the mirror. It called up memories of married bliss. Just so had Irene used to fuss over him. It felt good, to have a woman cosseting him. He studied her long lashes, spread like fans on her cheeks.

"You must go downstairs and be very biddable," Grace advised. "Ingratiate yourself with Lady Healy by making a fine renunciation scene. She will love to think she's saved you from ruin, But don't give up Mrs. Elton without a fight. I made her so beautiful, just for you." She patted the tie. "There. That's better. Away you go." She stood back to view her handiwork.

"Are you not coming?"

"My tender young ears must be spared. Be sure you tell me all the details later. I shall be dining alone."

Whewett was aware of a stab of disappointment. He was coming to enjoy Grace's easy, playful conversation. "Not again! No, that is too bad. I'll speak to her."

"Don't bother. I'm more relaxed away from her."

"I feel guilty that all the difficulties of the masquerade fall on you."

"I shan't mind. I'll have my dollie for company," she joked. "I call her Mrs. Elton, for she is very like my Mrs. Elton, with her blond curls. She'll be a lively partner."

"If she fails, you have plenty of liveliness to spare. Will you join us later?"

"If I am sent for. Otherwise I shall continue with the perils of Pamela. Frankly I am coming to despise her. I am half hoping Mr. B. will beat her with his sword hilt."

"He—"

She stopped him with a gimlet gaze. "Don't tell me. The book is boring enough when I don't know what is going to happen. Those pious, proper girls make for tedious fiction."

"Not only fiction. They're dead bores in real life, too. See you later, Doll."

Whewett went below to hear a diatribe on the vulgar, encroaching Mrs. Elton. He allowed Lady Healy to wring half a promise out of him that he would not marry her, but put up some resistance to allay suspicion. He did finally admit she was not the only lady he had in his eye.

Grace ate her potatoes and sausages alone, hid her bread pudding in the dustbin, and threw her warm milk out the window. When Molly came to inquire whether she had any laundry to be done, she decided to have her frock washed. The hem was muddied from playing with the geese, and besides, she wanted to have a bath while she was assured of an hour or so of privacy.

Chapter Eight

Molly felt obliged to help missie with her bath, and by the time Grace got rid of her, the water was growing chill. Her bath was more a dip than a luxurious soak, and when she emerged, she realized she would have to wear her own suit, as her dress was being laundered. She stood wrapped in a towel when the door to Whewett's door reverberated with his knock.

"Are you decent?" Whewett called.

"Stay out! I am naked as a needle!"

"Throw something on. I want to see you for a moment."

"It will take a while. I'll join you when I'm dressed."

While she stared in consternation at the door, it began to open. She clutched at her towel, but only a hand came through, holding a man's dressing gown. She took it and hastily pulled it around her, surprised at its elegance. The garment was richly patterned in deep hues of red and black, revealing a latent streak of the peacock in Whewett. The smooth caress of silk on skin felt luxurious. The robe fell to her ankles, and the fringed tie touched her toes when she moved to the door.

"What is it?" she demanded.

Whewett's gray eyes widened in surprise when he saw her. "Good God! You can't let Grandma see you like this! Why did you not buy yourself a proper dressing gown?" His tone was harsh, but his eyes betrayed some pleasure in her appearance. With her curls pinned loosely on top of her head and her face glowing from its scrubbing, Grace looked entirely delectable, but she did not look twelve years old.

"Buy a gown for two nights? What wicked extravagance! Is she coming right up?"

"Yes, she had a headache. She mentioned saying good-night to you before retiring."

"Oh, dear! You must go! I'll slip on my nightie."

Grace unceremoniously pushed Whewett into his own room and scrambled into her nightie. By the time Lady Healy arrived, she was in bed with her hair demurely tied up in bows, the doll beside her, and, unfortunately, one corner of *Pamela* protruding from beneath her pillow.

Before long, the dame espied it. "What's this? Reading something you shouldn't, eh? Humph, love stories. I suspected all along you had your head full of fellows. I hadn't realized you were turning into a woman already." Her eyes just glanced off Grace's bosom. In her thin gown, it was clear she was not a child. Grace slouched to conceal it as well as she could, but was not allowed to get off with that trick.

"Sit up straight, Augusta. It's nothing to be

ashamed of. I had breasts when I was thirteen. Stranger things will be happening to your body soon. Don't let it worry you. I never paid any heed to all that foolishness about not riding on my days. All stuff and nonsense. Well, I have rung a loud peal over your papa and half talked him out of the Elton creature, but I come to see he must marry someone. Have you any ideas?"

"Papa has good taste. He'll find someone."

"Of course he has. He married your mother. But he is getting old, and old men get silly. They take into their heads to marry a pretty young chit, to show the world they are still attractive. Very foolish things are done when a man is forty."

"Is—is Papa forty?" Grace asked.

"He soon will be."

They talked on for a while. No difficulties arose, as Lady Healy did most of the talking. Just before leaving, she said, "Would you like to come to Scotland and visit me sometime?"

"I would love to, Grandma."

"Invers could bring you. We shall think about it later."

This sounded sufficiently vague to agree to. Grandma gave Grace a hug and kiss before leaving. There was no repulsion at her swoop this time. She was just a lonely old lady, and Grace wanted to let her know, or at least think, that she was loved. "I'm so happy to have met you at last, Grandma," she said.

"I am a crotchety old lady, but you must not dislike me for that."

"What a thing to say!"

"I thought you might be afraid of me. I'm glad to see you ain't a widgeon. Stand up to me. That way we shall go on famously. Now I am off to bed. I hate being old. I used to dance till three, then be up riding at seven the next morning. Make good use of your youth, Augusta. It don't last long. You wake up one morning and see an old lady in the mirror, while your heart is still young. You only get to go around once. Isn't that a sad thing? By the time you've got a glimmering what the world is all about, you're too old to enjoy it. Don't I wish I were twenty again, with strong legs and a strong back. But I ain't. I am seventy-five and need my sleep. We turn back into babies before we die, sleeping and eating all day long. Brush your teeth, Gussie, and go to sleep."

"Good night, Grandma." Grace hopped up to open the door for her, and Molly came with a footman to remove the bath water. Grace watched Lady Healy depart, sad to see her hobble down the hall, leaning on her black stick. What unfulfilled dreams had caused that outburst from the old lady? Her life had been full—much fuller than Grace's own life.

She sat on the side of the bed thinking. It was fine to say make good use of your youth, but how was it possible in such straitened circumstances? Grace rose and went to the dusty mirror, to see a child staring glumly back at her, with the gloomy walls looking very like a prison behind her. She pulled the blue ribbons from her hair and tossed them on the dresser.

Whewett would be coming soon, and she began to dress. She put on her white lawn blouse, and as the room was warm, she did not bother with the jacket. Her skirt did not have to be hiked up when it was only Whewett who would see her. She ran a brush through her hair and, on impulse, piled it on top of her head, turning this way and that to study her appearance. If she could only get out of service, get some decent clothes, and meet a few gentlemen, she might make a match yet. But how could it be done? Her life, her youth, her precious one chance were all slipping away. She had to earn her bread, but she did not have to be a governess. Surely the world offered more exciting jobs. Acting, for instance . . .

She was a fair actress, to judge from the job she had done here. It was a shady career for a lady, but if a respectable marriage was beyond her, what did that matter? *You only get to go around once.* What a dreadful fate, to have your one round as a governess. If Lady Healy were in her position, she would not settle for so little. What an actress she would have made, with her dramatic height and commanding manner. She would have ruled the West End. But would a daub of a woman like herself be able to accomplish it? Not likely.

There was a discreet tap at the door. "Come in," she said.

Whewett stepped in and stopped dead. His last view of Grace had already upset him. In his mind he knew she was an adult, but it was a thing known without being felt. That first tantalizing glimmer was now revealed in its entirety. "Am I in the right place? I don't believe I recognize this ravishing creature." His eyes traveled slowly from the tip of her gleaming curls, over the swell of her breast, down to her toes.

She sensed his interest and said sharply, "It won't be for lack of looking!"

Her rebuke startled him back to business. "Why

are you dressed like that? Do you want to blow the whole thing?"

"Don't worry. I had my hair up in bows when she came."

"I trust you had on your jacket as well," he said. His eyes lingered on that blouse and the tiny waist below it.

"She doesn't suspect anything. We squabs of girls are early developers. We had a very interesting talk."

"That sounds ominous. You look—unhappy."

"I am. I would like to be put on the rack and stretched six inches."

"It sounds delightful. Many gentlemen prefer the pocket-size Venus, if this torture is designed for that purpose."

She tossed her head proudly. "It's not just that. Grandma gave me some excellent advice, but I don't know how to follow it." She walked to the bed and sat on its edge. "Have a seat, Whewett," she said, indicating the chair.

He went warily toward it. He was uneasy at being in a bedroom with what was very obviously a pretty young lady. As he had been in the habit of coming, however, he hardly knew how to extricate himself creditably. "What advice did she give?"

"To take life by the neck and throttle a good time out of it."

"She certainly followed her own advice."

"Tell me all about her," Grace said eagerly.

"She led the family a merry chase. There was a broken engagement or two, capped off with a runaway match with an ineligible officer of the Guards. He had the grace to die and leave her a romantic widow at eighteen. She went north, ostensibly to mourn, but I doubt there was much crape in evidence. The year was hardly out before she married Lord Healy and burned up the countryside with her pranks—happily ever after. The one lack in her life was a son. After a few miscarriages brought on by riding, she had a child, my wife's mother. My Augusta is her great granddaughter. Quite a lady, old Augusta."

"I knew she'd be like that," Grace said with a wistful smile. "I wonder what she would do if she were me."

"Some such thing as you are doing. She wouldn't stop at playing a child. She'd take to the boards at Covent Garden, get herself an influential patron or two—or ten."

"That is exactly what I thought."

"You're coming to know her pretty well."

"I am coming to like her, too. I think she is wise as well as wild. Whewett, have you often been to Covent Garden?"

"Frequently. Why do you ask?"

She stood up and turned a slow circle in front of him. "Do you think I might be an actress? Am I too dumpy?"

"What nonsense is this?" he demanded angrily. "Ladies do not turn actress."

"Oh, pooh! I am not a lady by anything but birth. I am a servant, to be ordered about by anyone who can pay me a hundred pounds a year. If I must work, I would prefer an exciting job. Do you think I am too short and plain to be an actress?"

"Yes! It is the most ridiculous thing I ever heard of."

She sat down, crestfallen at his vehemence. "You didn't have to be so positive about it."

"I am positive you are not going to be an actress, a byword in the clubs, a plaything for some doughty old duke."

"Much I'd care about that! I have a good mind to take my hundred pounds and go to London to give it a try. If I got some flashy, low-cut gowns and painted my face . . ."

"Stop talking such foolishness, Grace! What on earth did Grandma say to put such ideas into your head?"

Grace sighed wearily. "She said to make good use of my one chance. Imagine, I am having my one fling as a governess. Oh, it makes me so angry, I could cry."

"Being a governess is perfectly respectable."

"I'm tired of being respectable!" she exclaimed in frustration. "What do you know about being a governess? You're rich. You've always been independent. You've never had to stay up half the night with a whining youngster and get up again at seven, your eyes gritty with fatigue, to go back to work. You've never had to spend months doing work you hate—teaching arithmetic. I *hate* arithmetic. I hate Mrs. Bixworth and all the Mrs. Bixworths. The next job will be the same, or worse."

Her diatribe gave him some idea of her past and, worse, her future. He wanted to comfort her, but was restrained by reality. "Calm down, Grace," he said mildly. "It won't be the same. I'll speak to Mary. She has two nice girls, utterly unlike the Bixworths. Mary would be happy to have you."

"She must have someone already."

"She was complaining about her woman," he invented.

Grace looked at him with the dawning of interest. "What is she like, your sister?"

"Very nice. She certainly wouldn't work you night and day. She lives in a good style in Ireland, with plenty of horses."

"She wouldn't let me use her mounts."

"It could be arranged."

Grace shook her head. "I know you would arrange it if you could, but to treat a governess so would only lead to gossip in the neighborhood. I'm sure Ireland has its Mrs. Grundys, too. If I am to be a byword, I would prefer it to be in London, where they are used to such things."

"I don't want to hear any more about your becoming an actress," he said sternly. "I won't permit it."

He sounded so very much like her father in a rant that Grace had to stifle a laugh. But there was no point pestering Whewett with her problems, and she said no more.

"You have provided a valuable service for me," he continued. "I shall find a respectable post for you before we part. Now, the subject is closed. I have a bottle of wine in my room. We shall have a glass of wine and go to bed."

A conscious look entered his eyes, and Grace suspected he regretted his choice of words, but she ignored any ambiguity in the speech. "You don't have to assume responsibility for the rest of my life," she said.

"Somebody has to, as you appear to have lost the use of your reason." He strode stiffly off for the wine and glasses.

"We are not going to argue any more," she told him when he returned. "This visit is the highlight

98

of my day. I refuse to let you destroy it with your shockingly overbearing manner. You were more biddable with Grandma, I believe. She mentioned a renunciation of the Elton creature."

Whewett was happy to follow this topic. "It looms before me when I return home. I regret losing those gorgeous blond curls and blue eyes. I think Mrs. Elton and I might have gone on happily together, darting about the dens of London."

"She had that charming sense of humor, too. I could have grown accustomed to her as a step-mother. You would not have permitted her to beat me?"

"No, I would have done it myself, if you spoke of acting."

"There has been a moratorium declared on that subject. We are discussing Mrs. Elton, sir. She is only after your title, you know. You men in your forties turn very foolish. Grandma told me so," she added swiftly, when he glared at her.

"I do not happen to be in my forties."

"Only thirty-nine? I have wounded your vanity again. You are as sensitive as an aging lady. How old are you?"

"Thirty-five, fast pushing thirty-six." He looked closely to read her reaction, but saw only mild surprise.

"You have less than five years to find Gussie a decent mama, before you turn foolish and are picked off by the first pretty baggage that comes along. Forty is the turning point. One may do anything with a gentleman in his forties. I wonder if I might not manage to throw myself in the way of some foolish fellow past his prime. I could take my hundred pounds and to to Tunbridge Wells, where the gouty widowers are nursing their joints. What a splendid idea! With luck, I might even be a widow before I completely lose my looks."

"Grace," he said ominously, "You will not get the hundred pounds if this is how you mean to carry on."

"Welcher! Here you were offering me *more* a short while ago. What do I know about you after all? You might shab off and leave me stranded at the coaching house after I have served your purpose," she said airily.

"Very true, you know nothing about me, *including my age.*"

"Did you shave off a few years, Whewett?" she teased.

"Certainly not! But there are plenty out there who would do worse than lie about their age. You don't use enough caution for one in your position. Look at you this minute—with me, here in a bedchamber, unchaperoned."

"I never felt safer in a church. Besides, I put a chair under the knob after you leave," she added blandly.

"That strategy operates on the same principle as locking the barn door after the horse has bolted, I assume. Do you put a chair under the other knob as well, the door from the hall?"

"No, I doubt the groom who acts as butler is likely to come and ravage me. I'm sure he is well past such exhausting endeavors. And surely he would not be brass-faced enough to try it with my father right next door."

A reluctant smile alit on Whewett's face. "What is to prevent *me* from entering via the hall?"

"Your good sense, if not your paternal instincts."

"I do not feel any paternal instincts for you."

"Say gentlemanly, then. Unless you plan to go whole hog and murder me after you have had your vile way with me, you would be putting yourself in a precarious position. You want to be careful about keeping me in good humor, or I shall reveal all. Grandma's fortune would go whistling down the wind, to say nothing of your reputation if the story got wider circulation."

His amused smile showed no fear. "I didn't realize I had a potential blackmailer on my hands."

"*You* should be a little careful whom you take up with as well, milord," she cautioned.

"You are not quite so naive as I supposed," he replied, and filled her glass. He looked at his own, but decided against it. "Time for me to leave. Don't forget to put the chair under the knob, Grace," he said as he went to the door.

"You plan to sneak in by the hall, do you?"

"Is that an invitation?"

Grace gave a disparaging look. "How many years did you shave off? Five, was it?"

"I am thirty-five years and nine months, since it seems of some interest to you. I ought to mention, however, that we Whewetts are precocious. I married young and might turn foolish young, too. Tunbridge Wells, wasn't it, you mentioned as a good spot to pick up a flirt?"

"It was, but I should think a lightskirt would prefer a widower with no children, or the nursery already fledged. A half-grown daughter hanging on her arm when she goes up to London to make the next match might be enough to put her off."

"I am just at that awkward age, it seems. Too old
101

for a love match and too young to appeal to the fortune hunters."

"Five years will take care of your problem," she said.

"Good God, *my* fling is nearly flung, too. Ah, well," he said, hefting the wine bottle, "at least I am old enough to drown my sorrows. Good night, Grace."

Only after Whewett left did she notice he had stopped calling her Miss Farnsworth. When had it happened? During his tirade against the stage, likely. Anger would often blow away the proprieties. She felt a stirring of pity for him. His life was not very full, either. She wondered why he had never remarried. He must have been very much in love with Irene. Lady Healy would be able to tell her more.

Chapter Nine

At eight o'clock the next morning the family group met for breakfast. Grace took one look at her gruel and said, "I am not hungry today. Just tea for me, please."

She thought Lady Healy must be unwell. She did not protest or seem to notice when Whewett slipped an egg and toast on a plate and handed it to Grace.

The old lady sipped her drink, thinking. Later she said, "You must go into Wickfield for me, Alfred, and see Bronfman about a mortgage. Daugherty has only three thousand dollars in cash, but that need not beat down my price. Tell Bronfman I will take a mortgage for two thousand. A mortgage is a safe investment. I will let him have it at five percent. He would pay more at a broker."

"It will be a good selling point."

"I need that, for I am anxious to get home. I feel little shooting pains in my chest. I thought it was the flu coming on, but no cough developed. My physician at home, Dr. MacTavish, is excellent. He will have me feeling better in jig time."

"Very well, I'll see Bronfman," Whewett agreed.

"I shall stay quiet, write some letters. What will you do, Augusta? Will you go with your papa?" the dame asked.

"Yes," Grace answered promptly.

"No, you stay with Grandma," he said. Grace looked at him, surprised and offended.

"Take her along, Alfred. I shall be busy."

Grace looked at Whewett with renewed hope. He replied, "It is a nuisance having a child dragging along on business errands. Gussie will stay."

"Papa, please take me with you," Grace entreated, not believing he would consign her to such a tedious morning for no apparent reason.

"Not his time, dear. Perhaps tomorrow we can go out."

"Daugherty don't come till Friday," Lady Healy mentioned. "Tomorrow you and your papa can have a long drive. Don't pout and sulk, child. It makes you look like an ugly pug dog. Do you have a dog at home?"

The remainder of breakfast passed in harmless discussion. When it was over, Whewett took his leave. He directed a long look at Grace, which conveyed nothing to her, though she thought it was intended to.

"I'll set up my desk by the window so I can watch you skip," Grandma decided.

There was to be no escape. Lady Healy did as threatened. The rope was brought out, and the exercise began in a desultory way. When Lady Healy looked out, Grace speeded up, and when she was writing, Grace slowed the pace. At one point Lady

104

Healy set her letter aside and waved. Not thinking what she was about, Grace lifted a hand to wave back. The rope tangled in her legs and she pitched forward. It was not a hard fall, but Lady Healy became alarmed. It was very clear the old lady loved her, for she came pelting out the French doors at a gallop.

"Goodness, I hope you have not sprained your ankle!" Grace felt a perfect wretch to have caused such agitation. "Mercy, and it is all my fault, distracting you so foolishly. Can you hobble in and let us have a look at it? Lean on me, Augusta. Oh, dear, and Whewett not here. I'll send a boy for a doctor."

"I don't need a doctor," Grace said hastily. She could have walked unaided, but with the sun rising higher, she was relieved to have done with skipping. Were it not for the promised outing with Whewett, she might have taken to the sofa for a few days. She hopped in on one foot. Mulkins was called to fetch a stool. The ankle was examined with the stocking off. There was no swelling, but a red welt had burned a layer of skin away. The treatment was to send Mulkins off to make lemonade.

When the invalid had been made comfortable, Grandma handed her the Bible, while she resumed her writing. Grace leafed through the heavy tome, reading with very little interest of Abraham begetting Ishamel. When Lady Healy went to speak to Mulkins, Grace slipped quickly upstairs and brought down *Pamela*. With this tucked inside the Bible, she passed the morning more pleasantly than foreseen. At eleven-thirty Whewett returned, to be regaled with what Lady Healy called "Gussie's awful accident."

His head jerked toward Grace, revealing his alarm. "Are you all right?" He strode quickly to her and seized her hands, as though to satisfy himself that she was in one piece. When he noticed what he had done, he quickly dropped them.

"Yes, but I could only skip for ten minutes," she said in a doleful voice, while her eyes laughed over the top of the Bible.

"A pity. I see you are suitably occupied all the same."

"I'm reading Deuteronomy, Papa. Very uplifting."

Whewett suspected that pious smile and glanced down to see *Pamela* concealed behind its bulk. "You can certainly do with heavy doses of the Bible," he said dampingly.

"This terrible accident would not have happened if you'd taken the child with you," Lady Healy grouched, making clear he was the villain of the piece. After more regrets, she asked, "Did you speak to Bronfman?"

"He thinks the mortgage is a good idea, and of course he likes the five percent."

The sale was discussed till luncheon. Whewett offered his arm to Augusta to reach the table. With careful winces, she lagged along. "Don't overdo it, or she'll call in a sawbones. Did you hurt yourself at all?"

"It pains dreadfully," she told him, with such an innocent expression, he could not judge whether she meant it or not.

"Perhaps we should call a doctor," he said uncertainly.

Her smile twinkled mischievously. "Perhaps I should be an actress."

"On the other hand perhaps you should be thrashed. Allow me to get your chair, Grandma." He abandoned the invalid to shift for herself, which she did very well.

"May I have a wee glass of wine, Grandma, as I am feeling dizzy from my accident?" Grace asked in a wheedling tone.

"Ask your father. A sip of wine may settle your nerves."

"May I, Papa?"

His eyes raked her. "Certainly not."

"Papa!" she exclaimed, offended. Really Whewett was turning into a perfect tyrant.

"Half a glass won't harm her," Grandma said irritably.

"She is too young. Wine ruins a young lady's character. She will end up an actress, or something equally disreputable."

"Don't be such a gudgeon," Grandma replied angrily and gave up pretending Whewett had anything to say about it. She poured a full glass of wine and handed it to Grace. Later, she urged second helpings of dessert.

"You are forgetting we must watch Augusta's dumpy figure," Whewett said, pushing away the sweet tray. "After that clumsy fall, she cannot exercise. She should eat less, not more."

"You pick a fine time to exercise your discipline. The poor child needs some compassion."

"I am disappointed in my daughter's performance."

"I see what Irene meant now," Grandma said cryptically.

"What has my wife to do with it?" Whewett asked stiffly.

"She said you could be a perfect mule. The accident was *my* fault, and I find it incomprehensible that you choose this moment to be strict, when you are usually too soft by half."

Conversation was sporadic after this minor outbreak. "I managed to hire a decent nag at the inn," Whewett said. "It will make overseeing the estate easier."

"Well, Augusta," Grandma Healy said, "It seems you and I have nothing better to do than nap this afternoon. You may dine with us this evening," she decreed, with a challenging look to the father, who ignored her. "Take her upstairs for a nap, Alfred. You had best carry her to save that ankle."

"It's not broken. She can walk."

"Well, upon my word! I don't know what has become of your manners. Even Irene, for all her complaints, never said you was quite heartless."

"Irene did not complain. She had nothing to complain of."

While the two exchanged glares, Grace said, "I shall just rest on the sofa and read my Bible, if that is all right."

"It seems you have no choice, unless you are able to crawl up the stairs on your hands and knees," Grandma announced, and stalked from the room, her bosom heaving and her mind hatching a plan that would soon throw her guests into a conniption.

"You should abuse me more often," Grace said to Whewett, tipping the wine bottle to refill her glass.

"It can be arranged," he said in a thin voice.

"Why wouldn't you let me go to the village with you?"

"Never mind the attack, young lady. What do you mean by pretending you have hurt your ankle and lolling about indoors on a fine day like this, reading a trashy novel?"

"You forget I am not an energetic youngster who enjoys bouncing up and down in the sun for hours on end. You should try it some time! When I fell, quite by accident I assure you, and *did* hurt my ankle, I was delighted to get out of the sweltering sun. And don't bother ranting at me about trashy novels when you have read it yourself and told me the ending, too, in the most odious way."

"It wasn't the ending," he said. Whewett realized he had behaved badly and felt not only guilty but foolish. It was not today's stunts that bothered him, but Grace's notion of going on the stage. He could see its attraction to a provincial lady of little experience. The deuce of it was, he couldn't do a thing to prevent it.

"I recognize a diversion when I meet it, sir. Why didn't you let me go to the village this morning?"

"Because we should not be seen together. That pop-eyed woman from the coach—"

"I don't see why you cannot remember a person's name. Mrs. Sempleton."

"Yes, well you will be interested to hear I met Mrs. Sempleton. She is strangely interested in you. She told me she learned Miss Thomas has rented her house."

"Did she say where Thomas has gone?"

"She doesn't know yet. Give her another day."

"Is that why you didn't want me to go?"

"Of course. What other reason could I have?"

"I thought you didn't want my company."

He waved the idea away as foolish. "A pretty sly trick, making up to Grandma to get wine out of her."

"That's not why I did it. And why should you begrudge me that simple pleasure anyway?"

"I dislike to see you practicing your thespian skills. It revives a theme I hoped we had put to rest. Does that ankle really hurt at all?"

"I am suffering agonies but conceal it with my acting. I would be in bed this minute if you weren't too cruel to help me upstairs."

"I'll help you upstairs, if you like. And call in a doctor to leach you," he added, when her smile told him she had conned him again.

"I am quite comfortable here. I must recover for that trip you promised me tomorrow."

"The word *promise* did not arise."

"Whewett, you said you would!"

"Don't sulk, pug." He laughed. "I'll take you if you are a good girl and finish your novel."

Grace finished the book soon after he left. She went to the garden to hide the skipping rope in the bushes, to forestall further exercise. Then she walked around the house, exploring. The cellar door was open, and she went in, guiding herself carefully down the steep stairs to avoid real harm to her ankle.

Below it was dark and dank, with little to see. The light from the opening fell on the wine racks, and she went to examine them. John Brougham had kept a well-stocked cellar. There was even champagne. She and Papa used to have claret or port with dinner, but she had never tasted champagne. Before many seconds she had slipped a bottle under her arm and fled up the stairs. The kitchen door was ajar. Mulkins was not there, so she went in and up the servants' stairs to her room. She hid the bottle under her pillow, planning to have it that night.

And if Whewett was still in a snit, she wouldn't share it with him. He was acting peculiarly today. The strain of the masquerade was beginning to show, but she would not let him take it out on her. The greater part of the burden was hers. If anyone was to be allowed a fit of temper, it should be she.

Chapter Ten

Lady Healy rose after her nap and found Grace in the saloon, where she had gone to practice the pianoforte. After she had played a few selections for Grandma, the elderly lady said, "I have a very nice instrument in Scotland. How I should love to hear you play it for me, Augusta. You must do so when you visit me. I'll speak to your papa about your visit."

Grace nodded, believing this event was far in the future. She learned the startling truth as soon as Whewett joined them after completing his rounds. "Augusta and I have been chatting about her visiting me," Lady Healy began. "She is eager to come now that she and I go on so well together, Alfred. I have a notion why you hesitated before. You thought I'd frighten her, but it is no such a thing. We rub along fine. She has promised to play for me when she comes."

"Perhaps next year," Whewett said, stalling her.

Grandma was old and infirm; next year might not come for her.

As if reading his mind, Grandma said, "Next year might be too late. I want her to come now." Her arrogant face wore its commanding aspect, black eyes flashing.

Grace and Whewett exchanged a wary look. "You will be fagged after your trip," he said. "Best to let you get home and recuperate first."

"I would appreciate her company for the trip. And I do not get so knocked up during travel as you think. My carriage is well sprung. I take it slow, with plenty of stops to rest."

"Gussie is not ready to leave from here," was his next effort. "She has only a few clothes with her, and Invers is not available at the moment, either."

"Invers can join us later. Clothing will be no problem. We shall get her new ones. Her holiday is the perfect time for it, with no lessons to worry about."

"I had not thought to see her go off at this time," was Whewett's last, desperate objection.

"Well, start thinking about it. I want her to come. I insist," the old dame decreed. In her mind it was settled.

Whewett needed a breathing space to sort out the mess and entered into a discussion of Lady Healy's estate. A little later she suggested he change for dinner, and when he came down, he accompanied the ladies, one on each arm, to the table.

"I'm glad to see you ain't limping," Lady Healy congratulated Augusta. "The young recover quickly. I was tossed from a wild nag when I was fourteen. They thought I had broken my collarbone, but I went to dinner and danced for three hours

113

that evening. Perhaps I was a little older than four-teen. Lord, I'd give my right arm to be young again—be glad to be rid of it. The elbow aches like a bad tooth."

"Pretty young to be setting up as a flirt at fif-teen," Whewett quizzed her.

"Young? Why I had my first offer of marriage at fifteen, and half a dozen flirts before that. You're dragging your feet, Gussie."

"I am in no hurry to see Gussie grow up," Whew-ett said.

"She has to learn to handle the fellows. Let her start young, and when she's seventeen and ready to settle down, she'll know her way around. There is no saying she will settle for the first man she meets, like Irene. Now that I come to know her bet-ter, I see she has a deal more spirit than her mama. Pay no heed to your papa, Gussie. Find yourself a beau. I'll see if I can't help you in Scotland."

"It is not settled that Augusta is to go to Scot-land," Whewett pointed out.

Grandma just smiled in a condescending way. When the wine was poured, Grace surreptitiously slid her glass forward.

"I see what you are up to, minx!" Grandma laughed. "Never mind scowling, Alfred. She has to learn to drink, or she will make a cake of herself when she goes into society."

At the meal's end, Whewett was directed to bring his port to the Purple Saloon. Augusta tagged qui-etly after the grown-ups and sat in a dark corner to avoid detection. After a little business talk, Lady Healy turned to more personal matters. "Have you given any thought to your marriage, Alfred?" she asked.

"Yes, I think of it often."

"You should have been married years ago. You need a mother for your daughter, as well as a wife for yourself. Who else have you in mind besides that vulgar cit, Elton?"

"Mrs. Elton is not a vulgar cit," he objected.

"Title hunter! I know her sort. Up from the gutter by marrying some gouty old fool, and now she thinks to make herself a lady. She thinks to have easy pickings with you. You must not marry her, Alfred. Tell me who else you have in your eye. I want to hear what Gussie thinks of the ladies, too."

"As the criterion of acceptability appears to be my daughter's approval, let us hear which of my harem Augusta likes best," he suggested, smiling lazily.

"I like Lady Eleanor. She already has a title, so she cannot be after that," Grace said, tossing the ball back to Whewett to describe this fictitious lady.

"Let us hear about her," Lady Healy commanded.

"Unexceptionable," was Whewett's brief opinion.

"Pooh!" Grandma turned to Grace. "You tell me about her. I want to know more than the color of her hair, mind."

"She is not beautiful," Grace decided, "but I like her. She never tells me to run along, as Mrs. Elton does," she added with an innocent smile.

Grandma flew into delighted outrage. "I know how it was with that common Elton creature."

Whewett turned a stern eye on his daughter. "I am sure that Pamela—Mrs. Elton—never said anything of the sort, Augusta."

"Papa, what a whisker! Don't you remember the
115

time you were in the conservatory with your arms around her, and she—"

"I have no such recollection."

Lady Healy turned a fulminating eye on him. "You ought to be ashamed of yourself. Tell me a little more about Lady Eleanor, Augusta."

With an innocent face and a mischievous eye, Grace complied. "She is nowhere near so young or beautiful as Mrs. Elton. Her hair is not such a nice, shiny gold. It has a little gray around the temples. She does not wear such low-cut gowns, either, that show her shoulders and half her chest. She doesn't give me sugarplums to go away and play, like Mrs. Elton, but she is very nice. She takes me to church when Papa doesn't want to go and gives me nice books to read."

"She sounds very suitable." Grandma nodded approvingly. "What is her age, Alfred?"

"Forty-three," he replied without a moment's hesitation.

"That is a little old. Will she be able to give you a son?"

"Mrs. Elton is good at sons," Grace interpolated. "She has two sons by her first husband."

"Humph. By *somone*," Lady Healy muttered. "Still, Lady Eleanor is a little longer in the tooth than I like. Is there no one else?"

"There is a Miss Farnsworth living nearby," Whewett said, with a satirical lift of his brow in Grace's direction. She tried to frown him into discretion, but he ignored her.

"Let us hear about her," Grandma demanded.

"Not very attractive, I fear," Whewett began. "A rather dumpy girl and a shade impertinent."

"You always liked those stunted gels, like Irene.

116

I see a spark in your eye for this Miss Farnsworth. I daresay you don't mind in the least that she ain't up to your elbow."

"Actually she is nearly up to my chin."

"Is she wellborn?"

"I believe so—gently born at least."

"Fortune?"

"None. The father was improvident, and the lady has turned governess."

Grandma stared, bewildered. "May I know how Miss Farnsworth found her way into your list of eligible ladies? A dumpy creature of inferior stock and no fortune. Next you will tell me she has no character to boot."

"That is debatable," he admitted.

"What is your opinion of this paragon, Augusta?" Grandma asked, in accents of heavy irony.

"Papa is joking. The fact is, he has taken Miss Farnsworth in dislike for some reason. She usually gets the better of him in an argument, you see, for she is rather clever."

"Clever enough to have set her cap for Whewett!"

"Not in the least," Grace objected. "She would not have him if he begged on bended knee."

"How do you know this?" Grandma demanded and, fortunately, did not wait for a reply. "The woman is a sly rogue. It is a trick as old as Eve for ladies to let on they ain't dangling after gentlemen, hoping to pique their interest. Don't be taken in by it, Alfred. Gracious, are there no *eligible* ladies in Dover? Why are we discussing widows, elderly spinsters, and penniless governesses? Birth and fortune and character are what you want."

"And looks," Whewett added. "Pray do not marry me off to an antidote, if you please."

Grandma lost patience with him. "It is you who ought to come to Scotland. The lasses there are bonnie. The fact that they are mostly pygmies would suit you down to the heels, Alfred."

Before much longer Lady Healy said, "I am going to bed early. You may stay down and keep your papa company for half an hour, Augusta. Try if you can talk some sense into him. Come and say goodnight to me before you retire. I shan't be asleep. It takes me an hour to recover from Mulkins's hauling me about as she gets me into my nightgown."

As soon as they were alone, Grace turned a sapient eye on Whewett. "Why the devil did you bring my real name into the conversation?"

"For purposes of revenge, daughter. Why did you give her the idea I have been making love to widows in conservatories?"

"She is not at all missish, Whewett. She knows you have been making love to someone."

His brows lifted an inch. "You have a very improper notion of my character."

"I was only trying to add an air of authenticity to the romance. You *would* have been making up to her if she were my Mrs. Elton. It is what Papa did when Mrs. Nichols was after him. I adored her. All those lovely sugarplums! But still, I did not want him to marry her. I don't suppose Augusta really wants you to marry anyone, either. It was one of my great fears that Papa would bring a wicked stepmother down on my head."

"On the contrary, Augusta would be happy for a mother, but it is not a Mrs. Elton or a gray-haired Lady Eleanor who will make a good one."

118

"Nor a Miss Farnsworth, either, with her sly ways." Grace laughed.

Whewett examined her in an interested way, noticing that she was untouched by embarrassment. The idea of a match between them had not occurred to her, then. She was glancing at the bottle of port.

"May I have some?" she asked.

"Certainly not. You've had more than your one glass for today, young lady." He expected a pout or sulk and anticipated a few moments playful argument. It was enjoyable to have reached a footing of familiarity with a pretty young lady again. But there were no pouts, only a smug smile that made him wonder. "I would not want to undermine a lady's character by feeding her too much wine," he prodded.

A ripple of tinkling laughter rent the air. "Oh, I am already past redemption," she said, thinking of the champagne under her pillow.

The half hour passed pleasantly, and Grace left, slipping two glasses upstairs with her. She took them to her room before saying good night to Lady Healy. She then settled in with a new book to await Whewett. For half an hour she read and waited, wondering what kept him so long. An hour passed, and still he did not come. She was about to go downstairs after him when she heard the soft sound of footfalls in his room. She tapped on the door, wondering if it was his valet.

"What is it?" Whewett called through the door.

"It's me. I want to talk to you."

"It's late, Grace."

"It's only nine-thirty."

He unfastened the lock and glanced through the partially closed door. "Lord Whewett, are you locking yourself in to be safe from my advances?" she asked, her eyes wide with shocked amusement. Her hair was still done up in tails and bows, her child's frock safely in place, but since the night before, Whewett had been acutely aware of the impropriety in their situation. He had taken the decision not to enter Grace's room except in a case of necessity.

"What is it you want?" he asked stiffly.

She pulled the bottle of champagne from behind her back. "A party! I stole this from the cellar. I do hope you will join me. I don't want to drink it all alone. I have two glasses smuggled up as well."

Whewett felt the full allure of pleasurable misconduct that could be enjoyed secretly. He had to drag himself into line. "I don't think this is a good idea, Grace."

"Oh, do come. It is an excellent idea. I never tasted champagne in my life. I have been *dying* to try it and have been waiting an age for you to come."

He was hard put to find an excuse. "One glass," he relented, stepping in with more hesitation than real reluctance. Nine-thirty was demmed early to go to bed after all, and there was always the excuse of matters to discuss with his partner.

"Follow Grandma's good advice," Grace suggested with no air of constraint. "You only have one spin. Grab all the pleasures that offer. I may never have another chance to drink champagne—a whole bottle, I mean. I plan to drink all that you don't."

With this warning, Whewett imbibed a good deal of it in a great hurry. He was nowhere near bosky, but felt a pleasant glow. "Isn't it lovely?" she asked

120

two or three times. Her eyes sparkled with adventure, and the wine brought a flush to her cheeks. Whewett felt a compelling urge to pull the ribbons from her hair and loosen it around her shoulders. Those braids stood in the way of his pleasure, a constant reminder of her vulnerability.

Grace perched on the edge of the bed and lifted her glass, to admire it. He noticed that her smile was becoming wobbly. "How I should love to be rich and drink champagne every day. Do you drink it often, Whewett?"

"Very rarely. I prefer claret."

"You don't know how to enjoy your money," she said sadly. "I don't think you even know how to enjoy life, Whewett. I daresay champagne would not be so delightful if you could have it whenever you wanted, but I think it's lovely." She tilted her glass and drank. A drop of wine hung on her lip, and she flicked it with her tongue.

Whewett felt a stirring of desire. "I know what I would enjoy to do right now," he said, his voice burred with huskiness.

Grace set her glass aside with a sigh. "You don't have to tell me. We must figure a way out of this projected trip to Scotland."

She missed the quick look of surprise that flashed across his face. When he spoke, his voice was schooled to a normal tone. Much better to discuss business. "I have exhausted every excuse I can think of, and still she persists."

"I could become ill," Grace suggested.

Looking at her healthy young face, he said, "It would not fadge. Skipping has made you too robust."

"I could go with her," she said, with a tentative

peek to see how this was received. "I have nothing better to do. I like her and would not mind a trip to Scotland. Who would there be to tell her I am not Augusta? You would just have to make sure your daughter did not write to her while I was there."

"You indicated more than once an eagerness for our play to fold," he reminded her. "It is a visit of two or three months she has in mind, Grace."

Grace frowned as she imagined the future. "I could grow up a little over the months—lower my voice by the minutest of degrees and become more interested in the doings of ladies. She did mention finding me a beau."

"Aha! That's the attraction, is it? You mean to pose as an heiress and set yourself up with a well-inlaid laird. No, seriously, it is much too risky. Here you can come to me in case of any difficulty arising. I am bound to protect you. In Scotland you would be at her mercy. She would not deal easily with you if she ever learned the truth. It is a small world, you know. Someone from your own neighborhood or mine might be visiting and reveal your masquerade. She'd be furious. You'd find yourself clamped into prison, my girl."

"Perhaps you're right," she said reluctantly. "You always meet someone you don't want to when you are doing something wrong. It is practically a law. How shall we get out of it though? She considers it settled."

"I'll be damned if I know," he admitted. "We must cudgel our brains and come up with something. We can't offend her with a refusal when she's just told me Gussie is her heir."

"Some occurrence at Dover that I must attend?" Grace suggested halfheartedly.

"What could be important enough to prevent the visit?" he asked, drumming his fingers on his knee, while a deep frown creased his brow.

"Your imminent danger of falling into Mrs. Elton's clutches?" she asked, but in no serious way.

Whewett regarded her with a curious smile. "That has definite possibilities. Best let her suggest it herself, however. Grandma likes to be the instigator. Your role, daughter, will be to insinuate in that sweet childish way you have developed that whatever about your papa not wanting you to go, Mrs. Elton will be delighted at your absence. And of course you *do* hope that Papa won't be so lonesome that he invites Mrs. Elton to visit again. Yes, I think this has possibilities."

"I was only funning! It would never work, Whewett."

"I know it," he admitted.

"Perhaps if you became ill . . ."

"She'd only haul me off to Scotland for a cure—and a wife."

"Sickness, death, and accident are the only things I can think of that might put her off. You have not mentioned any relative being ill, and I cannot think we should go so far as to kill someone."

"An accident should be sufficient. Why don't I just break your leg or fracture your skull? You wouldn't mind, Grace? I'll pay you extra," he offered, and drained his glass.

"How much?" she asked, with a face quite serious, but for a certain sparkle in her eyes.

His gaze wandered from her head to her ankles. "Your head is worth little enough—quite empty. If

123

we must damage one of those charming ankles, however, that is a different matter." He set down his glass, rose, and made his bow. "I shall leave before I succumb to temptation."

"You didn't quote a price on the ankle," she reminded him.

"I was not speaking about the ankle."

"Then it is to be a fractured skull. I repeat, how much?"

"I wasn't speaking about the skull, either," he said. "Good night, Grace."

She listened as he slid the bolt on the door. If he wasn't talking about incapacitating her, what on earth—Grace gave a light laugh. So *she* was the temptation he referred to! Was it possible Whewett was trying to flirt? It must have been the champagne. She picked up the bottle and discovered it was empty, so she prepared for bed.

Chapter Eleven

It had been established that Whewett was to take his daughter out on Thursday but not at what hour they might leave and when they should return. Lady Healy informed them at breakfast that they might have the better part of the day.

"Mulkins and I will be selecting items to take to Scotland and packing them. I only want a few portraits and historical mementos of the Brougham family. At my age there is no point squirreling up a deal of sentimental rubbish."

She figured her work would not take more than an hour. The truth was that she felt dreadful and meant to spend the day in bed so Alfred would not take the notion she was sickly and use it as an excuse to keep Gussie from going to Scotland. She hoped to be revived when they returned from their outing.

"I have already found some things you will want, Alfred," she told him. "The painting of Irene from Mama's room, done by Phillips. I have collected up some of Irene's needlework for you and a sketch or two. They will be of interest to Gussie."

"I would like to see them," Whewett replied eagerly.

The items were brought to the Purple Saloon after breakfast. Grace's first interest was the painting of Whewett's wife. He must have been remarkably fond of her to have remained a bachelor for ten years. Grace thought she was about to see a stunning beauty, but from the canvas smiled a face no more than pretty.

"I see traces of her in you, Augusta," Grandma said fondly.

Grace looked in vain for this unlikely resemblance. Both were young, brown-haired girls with faces of an oval shape. Other than this, no likeness existed. She looked at Whewett and saw he was smiling wistfully at the portrait, so intent that he might have been alone in the room. How much he had loved his Irene! She felt a twinge of envy.

"It doesn't do her justice," Whewett said at last.

"It flattered her," Lady Healy countered baldly.

But the old lady usually contradicted any statement. Grace assumed it was a fair likeness. She was surprised that so little beauty had engendered this stoic, long-lasting devotion from Whewett. She was probably mistaken to imagine he had any flirts at home. Yet he hadn't really been angry at her inventing Mrs. Elton. In fact, he had seemed to enjoy the little game. Perhaps Whewett was ready to break free of Irene at last.

He examined the needlework and sketches, all rather indifferently done. "Augusta will want these," he decided.

"Now it is time for you to be off," Lady Healy

said. "I'll expect you home for dinner at six. Don't stuff Gussie up with bonbons."

As the two hastened upstairs to prepare for the day-long excursion, Whewett said, "Would it be possible for you to wear that convertible outfit you had on when we met? It will be an excellent chance for you to cease being a child for the day. In case we want to do something more adult, I mean."

"Precisely what I had in mind. My bonnet and slippers are still in your carriage?"

"Yes, you can slip them on there. Think what you would like to do and where. Of course Wickfield is out."

Grace scrambled into her old serge suit in two minutes. She met Whewett belowstairs before he thought it was possible. They had made their adieus to Lady Healy, so there was nothing to do but call the carriage and leave, their hearts light with the anticipation of a holiday.

"A whole day!" Grace crowed. "What shall we do?"

"My carriage and myself are at your disposal. Also my pocketbook. You have earned a good time."

"Are we too far from London to go there?"

He looked at her, astonished. "Was geography not on the Bixworth curriculum? We could not be there before nightfall. The gayer spots are all beyond our reach—Paris, Rome."

"Brighton?" she asked hopefully.

"That was my first idea. Unfortunately I have many friends and relatives who summer there."

"I can't think of any other place worth going to."

"I blush to confess the inferior destination I have in mind. Tunbridge Wells. As the scene of your next performance, it might be of some interest to you.

It's only twenty miles away. You can look over the gouty widowers and see if any of them appeal to you."

He watched, enchanted, as a smile warmed her face. "Lovely! I should adore it."

"Tunbridge Wells it is. Where will you transform yourself into a lady?" he inquired.

"Inside this carriage, right before your very eyes. A swish of the magic wand and, abracadabra, a young lady will appear." She pulled off her hat, slid the blue bows from her hair and shook it out, while Whewett regarded her, smiling. She couldn't unroll the band of her skirt while sitting, and the carriage was too small for her to stand up. She knelt on the floor and wrestled with it. "I have some idea how a dog feels, trying to catch his tail," she complained, but finally succeeded and sat down.

"There goes my pleasure in the trip," Whewett said. "Not another sight of the ankles all day."

"I hope I have not run off with a gazetted flirt! Where are you hiding my slippers and bonnet, Whewett? You are a very slow magician's helper."

He pulled the slippers from the pocket of the chaise, handed them to her, and looked with interest for another glimpse of the ankles while she put them on. She pulled a hand mirror from her reticule and instructed him to hold it while she combed her hair and pinned it up. It was difficult to do in a moving carriage, with only two inches square in which to see a corner of her face at a time.

"I shan't attract even a gouty widower with my hair falling about my ears," she said impatiently.

"There are bound to be a few blind ones in the lot," he consoled her.

"Please move the mirror to the left so I may see

the other side of my head. Oh, that's worse than the other! I look hideous. You'll be ashamed to be seen with me."

"You look charming. I shall be proud to be your escort," he said, tucking a loose curl up behind her ear.

"You must be one of the blind ones. Where are you hiding my bonnet? Let us hope it will cover this mess."

"Right here," he said, pulling it out of a paper, where his busy servants had concealed it. It had become crushed during its various peregrinations. Grace straightened it as best she could do and set it on her head, with a dubious eye on her escort.

"Well now, I *am* ashamed to be seen with that bonnet," he said. "Could you give it a touch of your magic wand?"

"As a matter of fact, I could." With a flourish she reached into her jacket pocket and brought forth the blue feather, its spine broken, so that it hung limply. "Oh, dear!"

"Can that wand make things disappear?" he asked hopefully.

"I'm afraid not."

"We'll try mine," he said, and before she knew what he was about, he opened the window and picked up the bonnet.

"Whewett!" She stopped him and put the bonnet on.

"We know where our first stop must be. I trust Tunbridge Wells has a milliner's shop," he said.

"You'll have to give me an advance on my pay."

"The bonnet will be a bonus. Meanwhile, would you mind awfully to take off that thing you are wearing? It doesn't do you justice."

She pulled it off and tossed it aside. "Grandma looked pale this morning," she said pensively.

"I wonder if she is feeling poorly. Those chest pains bother me."

"She is old to be racketing around the countryside."

"She only came to see where she was born, before she died, and to take home a few memories," Whewett explained.

"I suppose that's it. Phillips's portrait of your wife is very nice. You will be happy to have it."

"Yes, and Gussie will treasure the other things. She has very little recollection of her mother."

"How did she die?" The blunt question was out before Grace realized it might prove a painful one for Whewett. "Or would you rather not talk about it?" she added uncertainly.

"I don't mind. It was so long ago, it's almost like a dream now. Irene was far advanced in pregnancy. She had a dizzy spell and fell from the top of the great staircase to the bottom. We lost the child, and she died. It would have been a boy," he said in a quiet voice.

"It must have been horrible for you."

"Yes. I was away at the time, on business. Just at Dover, but when I got back, she was already dead. The last time I saw Irene, she was alive and laughing. It is the way I like to remember her."

Grace was ready to quit the subject, but Whewett continued his reminiscences. "Irene had a good deal of liveliness. She seemed little more than a girl herself when Gussie was born. Well, she was only nineteen at the time. Younger than you, Grace. Amazing to think she would be thirty-one now, if she were alive."

130

"You loved her very much, I think," she said softly.

"Yes." His voice sounded far away.

"That was such a long time ago. As you never chose to marry in all that time, I expect you never plan to?"

Whewett looked at her, surprised. "Why do you say that?"

"Well, at your age. . . . Oh, dear, don't fall into sulks on me, Whewett. I forgot your sensitivity. I only meant that you are no longer young. I mean—"

"There is no point scouring your mind for a euphemism. The fact is, I am old."

"I did not mean that! I only meant you would not have waited a decade to marry, that's all."

"I never actively looked for a wife, nor consciously decided not to marry, either. Naturally I want a son and heir. The right young lady did not happen to come along. At least—" He was smiling now, as though laughing to himself.

"What is the secret?" she asked.

"Nothing. Just remembering my foolish youth. I have an excellent memory. I can recall that far back," he added.

"I am happy for you, elephant. A love affair, I take it?"

He hunched his shoulders. "An affair, at least."

Grace threw up her hands in mock horror. "Please to remember, sir, you are traveling with an innocent child."

"I'll try to bear it in mind, Doll."

"I am not your daughter today. Remember that, too, if you can."

"Don't overtax this ancient brain."

They discussed their adventure, each claiming

131

the worst of the bargain. "But I rather enjoyed it, and today is fine," Grace said, as they drove into Tunbridge Wells. "Coming here with you reminds me of a trip Papa and I made to the Wells. He bought me a bonnet, too. Is that not a coincidence?"

As Grace was looking in her little mirror, she missed the scowl her thoughtless comment produced. Their first stop was a milliner's shop. Whewett entered with Grace, directing the groom to stable the carriage at the inn. Grace turned automatically to the plain round bonnets that would continue being useful to her as a governess. She set one on her curls and looked in the mirror without much interest or pleasure.

"Don't you think one feather would not be overdoing it?" Whewett asked hopefully.

"Why not? He who pays the piper calls the tune. You select me a feather." She ran an eye over the fancier bonnets, stopping when a high poke one with a pink ostrich plume caught her eye.

"Try this one," he suggested, seeing where she looked. "It will give you a few inches." She stood in front of the mirror, adjusting it. "Also a touch of chic," he congratulated. "Not to imply you need it."

"Gracious, no. There is nothing so elegant as a shiny serge suit. We want a chapeau worthy of it. I shall enjoy my one fling very well in this creation. Do you approve?"

"Very much." Whewett was no critic of ladies' fashions, but he knew the bright eyes and glowing smile of Miss Farnsworth were attractive. "If the pop-eyed lady from the coach could see you now!"

"*Sempleton*, simpleton. She has a name. Do you like the bonnet two guineas' worth? Shocking, is it not?"

"Highway robbery. We'll take it."

The clerk hurried forward. "Charming." She smiled.

"We think so," Whewett said, drawing out his purse.

"We don't get many men in the shop," the clerk said. "I have always noticed the ladies buy more dashing bonnets when their husbands are along. I'll just put this in a box." Behind the clerk's back, Grace looked at Whewett and smiled.

"No, my—wife plans to wear it."

"Then I shall put her old one in the box."

"I didn't wear a bonnet," Grace confessed. The clerk stared in disbelief as she took the money.

"You would think I had gone in without a gown," Grace said, laughing when they got outside the door.

"I made sure you would be complaining about her other outrage. Quite a leveler for you, being mistaken for my wife. You'll be scrutinizing your face for wrinkles tonight."

"I shall not! I'm afraid I would find them. We should have talked the clerk down a few shillings. Mrs. Bixworth always did."

"You get what you pay for."

"She would not have cut off the feather, stoopid!" Grace saw Whewett's jaw drop open and exclaimed, "Oh, I'm sorry. I should not have said that."

"It is always a pleasure to be insulted by a pretty woman. Doll used to call me a greenhorn when the merchants doused me."

"Really? I would never have used such language to my father. I thought you said she was shy?"

"Doll, shy?" he asked, staring. Then with a conscious look added, "She is not shy of me, her father."

"Lord Whewett, I think you have been conning me. Doll is not Augusta at all. Who is she?"

"Just a girl I knew once. You remind me of her at times, the way you toss your head when you are angry, and pout."

She regarded him in a measuring way. "I cannot believe my ears. Here I have been thinking you next door to a saint. I could not be more surprised if you had just told me you were Jack Ketch."

A touch of pink rose up from Whewett's collar. "She was just a friend," he said.

"A female friend for whom a gentleman buys things is often called another name. As you have just bought me a bonnet, however, we shan't become too specific." Grace shook her head and tsk'd. "I thought I knew you pretty well, too."

Whewett yanked at his cravat, trying to appear nonchalant. "Shall we, ah, go to the springs now?"

"Yes, perhaps you can pick up a replacement for Doll, while I select my widower. A good thing I have my new bonnet to seduce him."

"Watch your language, Grace."

He offered his arm to cross the street, and she took it as calmly as she would have taken her father's. It was not till they began walking that she realized how far she was from considering Whewett *in loco parentis*. A very different sensation came over her, in light of her new discovery. Whewett, despite his bland face and protective manner, was a flirt, and she had been entertaining him unchaperoned in her bedroom for the better part of a week.

Several ladies looked at Whewett with a lively

eye as they walked. Not old ladies, either. They also glanced at Grace with interest. There was a look on those faces difficult to describe but easy enough to interpret. "What does he see in that dowdy little squab?" the look said. He seemed to grow taller and more elegant as they progressed. Grace squared her shoulders and looked back at the ladies with a haughty stare.

There were more than ladies on the street. She soon realized that gentlemen as well were observing her and Whewett. He, too, was aware of the new sensation. It felt good to be walking along with a pretty woman on his arm again. He had been foolish to let ten of the best years of his life slip by. His fling was half flung; time was pushing hard at his back. He could feel it, but today, at least, he would live. A festive mood came over him, a mood to make a man do something foolish, like fall in love.

Chapter Twelve

They entered the Tunbridge Wells Pump Room and were confronted with such a plethora of gouty old gentlemen, presumably some of them at least widowers, that Grace gasped. "I feel like a very babe in here, amidst all this senility."

"Charming," Whewett answered. "It makes even me feel less senile. As we are here, let us try the water."

"It will taste wretched. What a poor advertisement all these frail invalids are for the place. It is a nurse they require, not a wife."

"Pick out the frailest of the lot, and you will be a rich widow in jig time."

They found an empty table and ordered their water. While awaiting its arrival, Grace took up a pamphlet from the table and read about the spa. " 'Famous since the seventeenth century for its chalybeate springs,' " she read. "What on earth would a chalybeate spring be?"

"No fountain of youth, from the looks of this crew."

"There is more. 'The waters were discovered by Lord North around 1625 and made popular by Queen Henrietta Maria, Queen Consort to King Charles the First.' Have you ever heard of Queen Henrietta Maria? I am not acquainted with the lady."

"I don't recall the name, but I have always felt sorry for her husband, losing his head."

"Ah, no wonder we have not met her about Wickfield. She is French. We might have known, with a name like that, she would be a foreigner. I should have thought Italian . . . 'Sister to Louis the Thirteenth.' Was he the Sun King?"

"No, ignoramus, that was Louis Quatorze. You didn't include history on the Bixworth curriculum, either? One wonders what they paid you a hundred pounds a year for."

"For my running ability, chasing those two wenches. How do you think I got those ankles you are always ogling?"

"I thought they were a divine gift, like long lashes or curly hair." His eyes lingered on her face as he spoke, and a smile curved his lips.

Grace felt disturbed at his examination and diverted him with a joke. "A pity my gifts stopped short of a dowry."

The water came in two large tumblers. They sipped tentatively. Grace wrinkled her nose and set the glass aside. "I thought warm milk, just on the verge of turning, was the worst brew ever invented. I was mistaken. I have no opinion of Queen Henrietta Maria's palate, I can tell you."

"This has got to be good for you, it tastes so awful," Whewett said, and drank a little more while Grace observed the patrons. "Have you picked out your prey?" he asked.

"I am undecided between the gentleman with the red nose and gray bagwig, and the little dandy who is ogling me through his quizzing glass. The bagwig is older and would stick his fork in the wall soon, leaving me a rich widow. I fear he is a drunkard, however, and might prove troublesome. The dandy is more elegant. He would be a tame pet, too. Which do you recommend?"

Before he replied, an aging female of formidable proportions advanced on the gentleman with the bagwig and sat beside him. "Now we know why the poor soul drinks," Whewett said. "Your choice is made for you, unless you wish to engage in maneuvers with that battleship that just hoved into view."

"I know when I am outclassed. It will be the dandy."

"You'll have easy pickings. He can't keep his eyes off you. I believe women really *do* come here to pick up a patron."

"It is a husband I am on the catch for, not a patron. Don't hand me over without some haggling, Papa. Hold out for a handsome settlement. What sum do you feel we should ask, keeping in mind my elegant new bonnet?"

"Some things are beyond price."

"True, and some men are so sly they can wiggle out of anything."

When he made no answer, Grace looked to see what had caught Whewett's interest. "If you tell me Mrs. Sempleton just walked in that door, I shall crawl right under the table. Is it her?"

"No, worse."

Before he could explain, a young gentleman advanced toward them, smiling broadly. "Alfred, old bean," he exclaimed. "Here's a surprise."

"Townsend, nice to see you," Whewett replied, with ill-simulated delight.

"What the deuce brings you to this godforsaken dump?"

Grace examined the fashionable gentleman; he was in his late twenties or thereabouts. He was not handsome but gave some illusion of good looks despite thin cheeks and a weak mouth. He was a tulip of fashion in a well-cut jacket of blue Bath cloth, an elaborately-tied cravat, and a pink flowered waistcoat. A quizzing glass was just being raised to his pale eye, to have a closer scrutiny of herself, she feared.

"Just passing through," Whewett answered vaguely.

This uninformative reply passed, as Townsend's whole interest had settled on Grace. He was trying to figure out whether she was a lightskirt and he had caught Cousin Alfred out in an indiscretion, or whether she was a respectable lady. The suit said lady, but the bonnet caused doubts.

"What brings you here?" Whewett asked.

"Mama is having her annual dose of the waters. I got stuck to bring her. Papa cleverly takes to his bed to avoid it. It is a yearly event."

Townsend returned his gaze to Grace. "I don't believe I have the pleasure of the young lady's acquaintance." The eye that turned briefly to Whewett was alive with curiosity. There was mischief too—a look that accused and congratulated and laughed all at one time.

Whewett began rapidly canvassing his few op-

139

tions. "Miss Farnsworth, may I present my cousin, Mr. Townsend."

"How do you do?" she said, blushing up to her eyes and giving Townsend the idea he had caught Alfred dead to rights.

"Miss Farnsworth," Townsend repeated, making the words a request for more information.

"Of the Exeter Farnsworths," Whewett added, choosing a district quite at random.

"Ah, the Exeter Farnsworths. Related to us?" Townsend asked, continuing his scrutiny of Grace.

"Connected to myself, on my wife's side," Whewett said.

"I see." Townsend nodded, not seeing at all, and suspecting he was being fobbed off. "Mind if I join you?" he asked, and pulled out a chair before they could object.

Meeting Townsend was bad; knowing his mother, the redoubtable busybody, was in the vicinity was worse. "Actually we are just leaving," Whewett said, rising up on the instant.

Townsend was grinning from ear to ear. "You've hardly touched your water," he pointed out.

"Wretched stuff. Miss Farnsworth, shall we go?"

"No need to rush off," Townsend said. "Since we are all here at Tunbridge Wells, let us arrange to get together. Lunch, perhaps? Mama is coming along any minute. She will want to meet Irene's— cousin, is it?"

"Niece," Whewett said wildly, before he remembered that Irene had neither brother nor sister. And if Townsend didn't know it yet, his mother certainly did. "We are due to meet Miss Farnsworth's companion in moments. We must dash. Nice seeing you, Townsend. Please give my respects to your mother."

Townsend placed a detaining hand on his cousin's arm. "Before you dart off, old chap, Mama will want to know what you are doing here. You know how women like all the details."

"We are on our way to Wickfield, to see Lady Healy."

"Are you indeed? I had no idea she was in England. I suppose it is old John Brougham's death that has brought her. Anything in it for your Augusta?"

"Lady Healy inherited the estate. It will be Augusta's one day. It is why I am on my way to Willowcrest now."

"Very wise. Have to butter up the old ones. How does it come Miss Farnsworth travels with you?"

Whewett hesitated an incriminating moment before he could think of a single thing to say. Grace spoke up. "I am going to see Lady Healy, too. With so many questions, you have lost track of the answers, Mr. Townsend. I am related to Lady Healy, too."

He considered this, then asked baldly, "Where do you live?"

"Here, in Tunbridge Wells," Whewett said hastily. "It is why I have come a little out of my way from Dover, to pick up Miss Farnsworth."

"I thought you said she was one of the Exeter Farnsworths," Townsend said, his smile growing broader as they sank deeper into mire.

"I moved," Grace said. "I live here with my cousin now, Miss Thomas. We really must go and pick her up, Lord Whewett."

"Mama will be here any moment. Sure you can't—"

"No," Whewett said, and taking Grace's arm, he fled out into the street, looking sharply about for Mrs. Townsend. She was nowhere in sight. They walked along at a rapid pace, though they had no destination in mind.

"Just how badly disgraced are we?" Grace asked, after they had hurriedly turned a corner off the main street.

"There is no disgrace at all. Merely I am sorry to have subjected you to an inquisition by Townsend and determined his arch-quiz of a mother shan't get at you."

"She has trained her son well. He didn't leave out any questions, did he? He didn't believe a word of it, you know. Why did you tell him my name? He takes me for a lightskirt, and it is the best thing for him to think, too, but I wish you had called me Miss Jones."

"Don't be foolish. Why should he think anything of the sort?"

"As he seems well-acquainted with you, I thought perhaps he knew of your affair with Doll, and likely others as well," she replied sharply.

Whewett took her elbow and resumed walking at a less harried gait. "Never mind putting it in my dish, miss. It was your rolling eyes at the bigwig and the dandy that gave him the notion you aren't quite the thing."

"Is he stupid enough to think I would be making up to them when I had attached such a distinguished patron as Lord Whewett? He must take me for a moonling."

Whewett turned a rueful eye on his companion.

142

"I come to realize the full odium of comparisons. Am I *really* a notch above the bigwig?"

Grace gave it careful consideration and said, "Yes, Whewett, and I think you might even be a notch above the dandy."

His chagrin restored her humor, and they continued their walk.

Chapter Thirteen

Whewett and Grace proceeded without encountering Mrs. Townsend. They were surprised to come upon a rocky, wooded area in its natural state in the midst of a bustling town. "I don't remember seeing this when I was here with Papa," Grace exclaimed.

"With luck you may find a duck pond to fall into."

"You could hold my head under while pretending to rescue me. I know you would like to strangle me, but it is in no way *my* fault that your cousin chanced along. Look, Whewett, benches. What a pity we did not bring a picnic lunch."

"I wondered how long we could go without your turning into a ravenous beast."

"I can hold off another hour. Let us look around." There was a plaque posted. "Wouldn't you know it, Queen Henrietta Maria again. She camped here for six weeks in 1630." Grace looked around at the not very magnificient surroundings. "One would think a queen could do better for herself. Commandeer a castle or inn. I daresay the town has encroached on her camping ground in the past couple of hundred years."

They strolled through the park, where sundry elderly people sat on benches, taking the sun or shade as struck their whim. "This is nice," Grace said. "If I save all my pennies, I can retire to this place when my working days are over."

The bucolic surroundings put Whewett in a languorous mood. "Have you given up on marrying a widower?" he asked idly.

"I have, and on a theatrical career as well. You were right. I didn't care for the way your cousin Townsend leered at me. I don't think I should like being a painted woman."

Whewett glanced down at her, wearing an enigmatic, small smile. "That is no reason you should give up entirely on your plan of marrying a widower," he said.

She noticed he did not say a gouty old widower, as they usually described her fictitious groom. It even darted into Grace's head that it was himself Whewett meant. Some air of consciousness about him suggested it, the way he looked at her so intently. The idea was so presposterous that she soon brushed it away. "Let's walk that way," she said, pointing to the left. "We can climb over those rocks and see what is on the other side."

Whewett went along in unimpaired humor, enjoying the outing. He usually strove to avoid gossip. Since that episode shortly after his wife's death when he had had the whole family in an uproar over Doll, he had lived a thoroughly respectable life. But today he didn't really care if anyone should see him and catch him out in an escapade. He half regretted missing Mrs. Townsend. He needed some excitement. He had grown dull living in the country.

"King of the castle," Grace announced, when they had reached the summit. "We can survey our domain from here. How very like my Miss Thomas that lady looks," she mentioned, pointing out a woman in a sun hat, knitting as she sat, occasionally looking at the scenery.

"She also resembles Mrs. Elton."

"Really? That is not at all how I pictured her."

"You see how you have wronged me."

"Wronged you? There is nothing wrong in dangling after an incomparable, so long as your intentions are honorable. Really that could be Miss Thomas. The bonnet is exactly like one she used to wear at home. Whewett, I am going to walk closer and see if it is. We never discovered where she was gone."

They clambered down the slope. He was sure Grace was seeing what she wanted to see, but when they were within a few yards of the woman, Grace let go of his arm and flew forward, calling. "Miss Thomas, it *is* you!"

The woman looked up in alarm, stared silently a moment, then held out her arms. Grace rushed into them, hugged her old friend, and sat beside her on the bench with a dozen exclamations of surprise and delight. Whewett looked on, strangely disappointed. He had been looking forward to this private day with Grace. He knew it was well for her to find her friend, but he wished it could have happened later. He hid his feelings, however, and walked forward to be presented.

To say Miss Thomas was surprised to find herself being made known to Lord Whewett would be understating the case. She knew nothing of him, had never heard his name, but that Grace had fallen into a relationship with a lord certainly amazed the good woman. "How do you do?" she said, too stunned to say more.

"Don't *you* think I have become a fallen woman, too, Thomas," Grace said in vexation. "Lord Whewett is not my beau, appearances to the contrary. I am working for him."

"I see," Miss Thomas said weakly, wondering what position she filled that she behaved so freely with her employer. "What sort of work do you do for Lord Whewett?"

"I pretend I am his daughter."

Miss Thomas stared, trying to make sense of it. Failing this, she became angry. "Do you indeed, missie? I should not think you fool anyone, unless his lordship was married while still in short coats."

"You misunderstand, Thomas. It is *I* who wear short *skirts* for the job. I dress up as a child and spend my days skipping in the garden and playing with a doll and drinking sour milk."

"Where do you spend the nights?" Miss Thomas demanded bluntly. She cast an eye full of suspicion on the gentleman, who stood overwhelmed with shame.

"Shame on you," Grace chided her old friend. "I spend the nights in my room, from eight-thirty onward." She went on to explain the masquerade, and how it had come about.

"You'll be fortunate if the pair of you don't land in Newgate. If you found yourself in a pickle, Grace, why did you not come to me?"

"I was on my way to you. What else would I be doing in Wickfield? Don't be vexed with me, Thomas. There was no harm in it. You can see what a perfectly honorable gentleman Lord Whewett is. He will be shocked at what you have been hinting. He thinks of me as a very daughter, don't you, Whewett?"

"I assure you there has been no impropriety," he told Miss Thomas earnestly.

"I know Grace would not stand still for that, but you must own, her reputation would suffer if this should ever get out."

"Why should it?" Grace asked. "Lady Healy was with us the whole time. It is not as though we were unchaperoned."

"Where is she now?" Miss Thomas asked.

"At Willowcrest, preparing for her return to Scotland. Oh, and the worst thing, Thomas, she wants to take me with her."

"It wouldn't surprise me much to hear you plan to go."

"No, Whewett does not think it a good idea. May I come to you after she leaves, till I find a new position?"

"Certainly. You must," Thomas answered, with a jealous eye to Whewett. The impracticability of this scheme was not long in occurring to her. She was visiting an elderly cousin who lived in small quarters, quite retired in Tunbridge Wells. Miss Thomas was at this moment having her one outing of the day, while her cousin slept. The remainder of her day was spent tending the cousin's sickbed. Really a visit from Grace would be extremely inconvenient.

Grace was familiar enough with her old friend

that she knew at once there was some difficulty and was sure enough of Thomas's regard that she felt the problem to be one of lodgings. "Where is it you are staying?" she asked.

"In an apartment with my cousin, on High Street."

"How large an apartment?"

"Large enough. You can share a room with me."

"Yes, of course," Grace said promptly, but she felt this option was no longer open to her. Bad enough to batten herself on Thomas; she could not do so at the small apartment of a total stranger. "Give me the address," she said, for of course she must write and explain to Thomas, whatever decision she ultimately took. Thomas wrote it down for her.

"Let us walk you home now, so that I will know exactly where to come," Grace suggested.

Miss Thomas was not eager to show Whewett the mean establishment. It might give him the idea Grace had no respectable connections and was poorly protected. "I don't plan to return for a while yet. This is my daily outing. I usually stay a couple of hours."

"Come to lunch with us, then," Grace urged.

"I have lunch with Cousin Marion when I get back. It will be all ready," she lied.

"How long do you plan to remain at Tunbridge Wells?" was Grace's next question.

"I've let the Wickfield cottage till Christmas. Why do you not stay and chat with me, and let Lord Whewett pick you up later?"

Grace hesitated a moment. "This is our little holiday," she said. "We came together, you know, and what would Whewett do alone for two hours or so?

Besides, we are just on our way to lunch. I am starved."

"A lady is never starved, Grace," Thomas scolded. "She may feel a little peckish."

"Well, I am feeling very peckish."

"As usual," Thomas said, shaking her head.

Whewett offered to amuse himself while the ladies had their chat, which did something to raise Thomas's opinion of him. They all remained together chatting for another half hour. Thomas had to be regaled with the story of Grace's departure from Bixworths', and the ubiquitous Mrs. Sempleton. She noticed during the visit that Whewett regarded Grace with a fond smile seldom seen on the face of any but lovers. Once she took the idea he was in love with her ex-charge, he rapidly became an excellent fellow.

She suggested a short walk, and while Grace took a run ahead to drink from a fountain, Miss Thomas put the time to good use. Whewett was expertly quizzed. Before they parted, she knew all there was to know, including the fact that he was defensive regarding Grace's part in the masquerade. Proprietary did not seem too strong a word for his attitude. He spoke of his sister in Ireland, who would like to hire Grace. He also said to Thomas something he had never mentioned to Grace, namely, that Miss Farnsworth should accompany him to Downsfield to await his sister's arrival. When he inquired obliquely whether she herself would be available to accompany them, Miss Thomas knew he had no intention of doing anything but marrying Grace. A girl he hoped to see as his niece's governess had no need of a companion. Miss

150

Thomas had to decline the invitation, but she felt sure he would come up with a replacement for her.

Grace leaned over to give Thomas a last hug before she and Whewett left. Thomas whispered in her ear, "I like your young man excessively. Don't let him slip through your fingers."

"Thomas!" she exclaimed. "What are you think ing of?"

Thomas just smiled and nodded her head sagely.

After they had strolled away, Whewett said, "What did she say to startle you?"

Grace felt a warm flush suffuse her cheeks. "She said she thinks you're very nice."

"Your reaction is hardly flattering. You seemed utterly astonished that she should approve of me. I must own, I never felt so small in my life. She thought I had been carrying on with you. It is only what anyone would think, I daresay."

"She may have thought so for a moment. She doesn't now. Where can we go to eat that we won't meet Mrs. Townsend?"

"That presents no problem. She pinches every penny till it squeals. We have only to find the most expensive place, and we will be sure to evade her."

They went to the best inn, where Whewett hired a private parlor. "We have already been found out by my family and what you consider your family, I should think. Any chance Mrs. Bixworth will be visiting the Wells?" he asked.

"After meeting Miss Thomas, I rule nothing out. I must warn you in advance, Whewett, if we *do* meet her, I plan to introduce you as my fiancé, to watch her stare. How I should love to do it."

"I am at your service," he bowed.

"It would serve you right for telling your cousin

my real name. Only think if I should run into Townsend again sometime."

"If it ever happens, surely it will be better for him to call you Miss Farnsworth, unless you plan to become Miss Jones on a permanent basis."

"That's true. I might meet him sometime if I work for your sister. How wide-awake one must be when she enters into a life of deceit." Grace frowned at the pitfalls awaiting her.

"You will want to order a good meal, to keep your strength up. Shall we go whole hog and have champagne? Our one fling," he urged, "let us live it up."

"Could we, Whewett?" she asked, eyes glowing.

"Why not?"

"You prefer claret."

"Today I feel like champagne."

They drank champagne and talked very foolishly about a great number of things over their dinner. Eventually, however, they had to discuss less pleasant matters than what Grace would do if she were rich and what Whewett would do if he were king. "Grandma plans to leave very soon," Grace mentioned over dessert. "We still have not thought how to tell her I am not going with her."

"I'll just have to put my foot down, assert my rights, and say I won't let you go."

"She might take it out on Augusta. All our work will have been for nothing."

"I doubt if she would, but she would certainly take it out on you if you went and she learned the truth."

With a dismal thought of her future, Grace said, "I half wish I could go."

"Miss Thomas is expecting you to join her."

"That's true," Grace said with a feeble smile, for of course she could not join Thomas.

"I don't think you will be comfortable there, Grace," was his next speech. "Miss Thomas is pretty fully occupied. You would do better to come to Downsfield with me and await Mary's arrival there."

"That would put your sister on the spot. She would feel some obligation to hire me, whether she wished it or not. Nothing is more likely to make her dislike me. Besides, how could I go to stay with a widower? It would look very unconventional."

"I have relatives. I can find someone to chaperon us."

"So much trouble is not taken for a governess. People would talk. I should think Lord Whewett is discussed a good deal at Dover."

"I live removed from the town. I trust my past behavior hasn't made me quite a byword."

"Ah, the sensitive feelings are bruised again. I wonder if you aren't part orchid. They fall apart if you look at them."

"I can't just leave you at loose ends, Grace. We must find some suitable place for you. Your Thomas is kind, but living with an invalid in a little apartment—I know! I'll take you to my Aunt Gertrude in Dover."

"Does she require a companion?" Grace asked with interest.

"No, she has a husband and family."

"If she doesn't require anyone, why should I go there?"

"Because it is close to Downsfield—convenient," he added.

"To wait for Mary." She nodded. "I ought not to

call your sister Mary, but I hear you do so, and have caught the habit. You will find it hard to credit, I once had some notions of propriety."

"You behaved like a very proper young lady on the stage to Wickfield. I noticed it particularly. Shall we go? It is a longish drive home."

"I'm sorry our holiday is nearly over. I enjoyed it very much. Thank you, Whewett."

"Thank you, Miss Farnsworth. I enjoyed it, too."

They continued to enjoy the dregs of it on the return to Willowcrest. As they approached Wickfield, Grace again effected the change to Augusta. She had no sooner got her hair pulled into tails and the ribbons tied on than the carriage rolled into town. The first person seen on the street, with a basket over her arm, was Mrs. Sempleton. "I don't believe it!" Whewett exclaimed, pointing her out.

Grace ducked her head, while Whewett returned the woman's wave. "She lives on the street," he scolded.

"She is going to see us together before we get out of this place. Are we past?" Grace asked.

"Yes, get up. We should let her see us together. It would make her day, trying to figure it out."

"Why should we cavil at a Mrs. Sempleton, indeed, when everyone else has seen us? If we meet her again, I shall wave and tell her you have adopted me."

Whewett smiled. "I wished, when you told her on the stage that girls talk too much, that I could know you better. Did you mean it for a leveler?"

"Of course I did. You must know a lady never insults anyone accidentally."

They fell silent till they were nearly home, then Grace asked, "Do we tell Grandma we went to the

Pump Room and the park, and not mention the Townsends?"

"That will be best. The connection is on my own side, not Lady Healy's. There is no reason Mrs. Townsend should be in touch with her," he said unconcernedly.

How should a widower who took little interest in gossip suspect the curiosity of an arch-quiz, or know to what lengths she would go to ferret out news and cause mischief?

Chapter Fourteen

Over dinner Lady Healy demanded all the details of their outing. At eight o'clock, she informed a bright-eyed Grace that she looked burned to the socket and must retire early. The hour till Whewett was sent abovestairs passed pleasantly in memories of her day. As soon as she heard footsteps in his room, she went to the door and tapped before turning the knob. To her surprise, the door was locked. "What is it?" Whewett called, without even approaching the door.

His voice sounded withdrawn, emotionally distant. Grace was aware of a new sense of impropriety in the situation herself. It was having been an adult all day that accounted for it. "Is everything all right?" she asked.

"Of course. She suspects nothing. How should she?"

"I don't know. You sound—strange."

"I am tired. I'm going straight to bed. Good night, Grace."

Her first reaction was annoyance, which soon dwindled to sadness. "Good night."

She was acutely conscious that night of the unseemliness of sleeping next door to Whewett without even a lock on her side. He must find her farouche, to say the least. The oddest thing of all was that until this evening, the arrangement had not struck her as questionable. Even when he had inquired once if she was inviting him to sneak into her room after the household was asleep, she had only laughed. But the question showed that it had at least occurred to him. When she eventually fell into a fitful doze, it was of their outing that she dreamed. Much later she awoke and saw a beam of light beneath Whewett's door. She heard a measured tread that told her he was pacing. He, too, felt this new strangeness in their relationship and a reluctance to defy convention.

In the morning she examined his behavior closely to see if he revealed what thoughts had kept him awake the night before, but with Lady Healy at the table, he behaved exactly as usual. After breakfast Whewett took Daugherty over the estate, and Grace went for a brisk walk, as she had carelessly "lost" her skipping rope. She was not within view of the road when an antique black traveling carriage drove up to the door, nor would she have recognized Mrs. Townsend in any case. Half an hour later Grace was completing her circuit when the carriage left. A black bonnet within suggested an aging female caller. Some old friend or neighbor of Lady Healy, she thought, and went lightly into the hallway, calling "Grandmama!" in her childish voice.

"Come in here, miss. You have some explaining to do," Lady Healy called. Her voice alerted Grace to trouble.

A glance into the Purple Saloon sent her heart sinking. There on the table sat her new poke bonnet with the pink feather. Beside it rested her slippers, left in the carriage the day before. Lady Healy regarded these items, her face set in a grim, horrible frown. As Grace watched, the dame's one free hand went to her hip in a bellicose attitude strangely at odds with her years and her cane.

"Yes, ma'am," she answered timidly, and walked in.

"Will you be so kind as to tell me what these articles were doing in Whewett's carriage?" she demanded.

Grace swallowed twice, while her mind worked feverishly. "How did you find out?"

"I'll ask the questions, miss!" She also went on to give the answer. "Mrs. Townsend has told me the whole, so there is no point in lying. That takes you by surprise, eh?"

"Yes." Her answer was an echo of regret. How much had Mrs. Townsend learned? The woman had not seen her.

Lady Healy's next speech gave her a rush of hope. "Never mind trying to protect your papa. He met that Farnsworth creature in Tunbridge Wells. I know the whole, except what he did with you while he cavorted about the Pump Room with that hussy. I know you were not with them. And why did she leave her things in the carriage?"

"I—I believe he bought Miss Farnsworth a new bonnet," Grace said. No plausible explanation for the slippers occurred to her.

"The gudgeon, letting himself be fleeced by a trollop. But where were *you* all the while, Augusta?"

"I was in the park." The important thing was to conceal the masquerade. Whewett must make his own excuses.

"Alone?"

Those black eyes seemed to bore right into her soul. "Yes."

"Your father abandoned you *alone* in a public park while he made a rendezvous with a lightskirt? Is that what you are telling me, Augusta?" An awful wrath was gathering in the old lady. Grace wished to decrease it, but hardly knew how. Lady Healy ranted on, gathering steam as she advanced. "I'll not leave your fortune in his hands. He has no more sense or common decency than a dog. I shall appoint the court as guardian of your inheritance."

Grace had a strong feeling that Whewett would hate this. It would be a blow to his self-esteem, to be held untrustworthy, publicly deemed an improper parent. It was also unfair, for whatever else he was, he was an outstandingly good and loving father. High spirits and daring in Augusta, on the other hand, had never been entirely unacceptable to the old lady. "No! Papa would never do that—" Grace looked fearfully to assess the degree of danger and punishment that might proceed from a different version of the afternoon.

"Aha! I knew it! Whewett ain't a complete ninnyhammer. Never was a womanizer. Tell the truth now, missie, and it had best be good!" The dark eyes examining Grace held a greedy light. "What was the bonnet doing in the carriage?"

"It was me. I wore the bonnet." The dark eyes

glowed with satisfied shock, encouraging her to continue this tack. "For a lark, you know. I—I convinced Papa to buy it for me, when we went in to buy a present for Invers."

"You did not wear such a bonnet in public in short skirts. What did you wear with it?"

"A long skirt. I—I found one in the clothes press in my room and wore it pulled up till I was in the carriage. And the slippers—we bought a used pair at Sempleton's Cobbler's shop in Wickfield, to complete the outfit. It was just a little masquerade, Grandma, for fun. It's *my* fault. I talked Papa into it. No harm was done."

"You are a saucy minx, Augusta. You have caused a good deal of gossip with this prank. I know what it was all about. You wanted to go into places a young lady would not be allowed—to drink wine in a fancy inn and make a cake of yourself. Did you have wine, eh?"

"Champagne," she admitted in a small voice, with her head bent to denote shame.

Lady Healy was not at all horrified, nor one bit angry. She could hardly keep from laughing aloud. Here was a reincarnation of herself, a madcap ready for any rig. Of course some punishment must be meted out for the looks of it.

"Baggage! This will not go unpunished. I ain't a cloth-head, even if your papa is. He ought to have a good whipping as well."

As well? Grace looked up with real fear, in light of this new twist. She didn't doubt for a moment that Lady Healy was capable of it. "Papa never whips me!"

"I know it well. That is exactly the problem. You

160

deserve a stick across your back, and you shall have it."

Grace regarded her warily. She was old, her arms weak. Her blackthorn stick jiggled with the effort of standing. She could not hit very hard. It would be a tap, and there would be a gift afterward to atone for it. "You'll feel this," she warned, lifting the black stick. The unfinished piece of wood was blistered with knobs and looked a hefty weapon.

Grace gauged her opponent and alit on an alternative punishment. "Hit me, then. That is better than being locked in the attic."

Her ruse worked. An expression of relief flew to the sagging face that looked down on her. "Is that what you fear most?"

Grace lifted her chin boldly. "I'm not afraid of anything."

"Except being locked in the attic." Without further conversation the groom-butler was summoned. "Lady Augusta will be locked in the attic till dark without food. Take her away."

The dame turned on her heel and stalked to the window, her heart beating wildly with excitement. She wanted to run after Augusta and hug her, but discipline was clearly required here. The unwonted turmoil caused a twinge in her chest. Wayward girls were the devil of a nuisance, though she had no use for any other kind. Could she handle Gussie in Scotland? MacTavish was forever cautioning her against undue excitement. But of what good was life without it?

Grace had no opportunity to garner up her creature comforts before she was shown up into the sprawling attic of Willowcrest. The attic, a vast unpartitioned expanse with sharply slanting walls, was hot and close. Rectangles of light from the windows showed dust motes suspended in the air, but beyond these patches, the room was forbiddingly dark. Her first act was to look for a means of escape. The butler had locked the one door to the story below. It must be a window, then. She ran from one to the other, examining them, noticing with dismay that they had actually been nailed closed, with long, sturdy nails, to prevent banging or drafts.

There was just one that had been secured with wooden pegs, perhaps to permit access to the roof below. She jiggled the pegs out without much trouble and slid the window up. She leaned out, gasping for fresh air. There was no immediate danger of falling the several stories to the ground, for the gabled window was only one story higher than the roof below. The major difficulty was that if she hopped down to the roof, she had no means of regaining the attic, and she was not at all sure that being stranded on an open roof in the baking sun would be better than being inside. No tree was close enough to permit descent by that means, or even to provide shade.

There was nothing to do but await Whewett's return. To pass the time she had a look at the attic's contents. Ancient gowns and jackets smelling of camphor and dust beneath their coverings held little appeal. Chairs with one leg broken, lamps with a cracked chimney or base, blackened iron pots, and odd pieces of lumber provided slim prospect of entertainment. Before long she was back at the window, trying to decide how to contact Whewett and warn him of what had happened before he entered the house. She could see the stable from here; she must take up a vigil at the window and call to him as he came home. He had left three hours ago. He would not be much longer.

She clambered to the window ledge and sat with her legs dangling outside to wait for him. From her perch, the countryside looked like a patchwork quilt done in shades of green, with an occasional house, barn, or road to relieve the monotony. In less than thirty minutes she spotted Whewett approaching the house. He was with Daugherty and Bronfman. She waved her hand wildly, but the men were talking and did not chance to glance up at the window. Desperate to draw his attention, she jumped down to the next roof and hurried to the edge, calling as loudly as she dared when they drew near. The three men looked all about and finally discovered her, leaning over the edge of the roof.

"Good God, she'll fall and kill herself!" Bronfman exclaimed.

Whewett just looked, speechless. "Papa, I must speak to you *at once*," Grace called. She waved at the other men with a sheepish smile. "Grandma locked me in the attic," she said.

"You gentlemen run along inside. I shall be in presently," Whewett said. "It will be best not to mention this to Lady Healy," he added. They spoke some joking words of agreement and left. Whewett looked up and called, "Stand back from the edge of that roof before you fall and break your neck!"

"The worst thing, Whewett. She has found out about yesterday. Mrs. Townsend has been here."

"What does she know?"

Grace briefly outlined her ruse. "Don't spoil it," she warned. "She is livid with you, too. She is threatening to use her cane on us."

His jaw tensed, and his voice lashed like a whip. "Did she touch you?"

"No!"

"Stay there. I'll be right up. And get away from that edge."

Whewett disappeared. In less than a minute he strode briskly into the Purple Saloon, where Lady Healy sat with Daugherty and Bronfman. "I'll have the keys to the attic," he said, extending a hand peremptorily.

"I'll speak to you later, Master Jackanapes," she replied.

"The keys, Lady Healy. *Now!*" The word was a bark.

The dame's notions of propriety did not permit squabbling in front of the lower orders. She could bring Whewett to heel more satisfactorily later. "The butler has 'em."

Whewett stalked into the hallway and got the keys. He mounted the stairs two at a time, wrenched open the attic door and continued his swift ascent into the attic. In his warm condition the heat hit him like the blast from a furnace. He uttered one of those expletives that lurk at the bottom of all men's vocabularies, then ran to the window. Grace stood beneath him on the roof, looking up, and wondering how she was to get back inside. "Whewett!" she exclaimed in relief.

"Are you all right?" He had his foot on the windowsill, prepared to join her.

"Don't jump!" she shrieked. "We'll never get back inside. Can you help me up?"

"That woman is insane! It's hot as hades up here. You'll be prostrate with the heat. Here, give me your hands."

164

He got a firm grip on her wrists and began lifting her up. With the poor leverage the window allowed, however, it was impossible to haul her more than six inches off the roof. "You're pulling my arms out of their sockets," she complained. He released his grip immediately. The suddenness of the release sent her sinking on her knees. In a split second there was a thump beside her as Whewett landed on the roof.

"Are you all right, Grace?" he asked, leaning down to help her up. She saw the fear and anger in his eyes and heard the rough edge of concern in his voice.

"My skipping ankle has had another wrench," she said with a cringe as she tried to put her weight on it. His hands, around her waist from helping her up, enfolded her, pulling her against him, where her head nestled against his chest. The strength and protection of his arms were welcome after her ordeal. She was ambushed by the temptation to stay there forever, safe from the ugly present and worse future. For a moment she relaxed. She felt one hand move to her head, stroking her hair in a caressing way that went beyond mere comforting, and felt flustered.

She pulled her head back and discovered a peculiar expression on his face—a softening of the harsh lines just seen. "You shouldn't have jumped, Whewett. We'll never get back in now," she said breathlessly.

"Are you all right? Did she hurt you? How's the ankle?"

Grace detached herself from his arms and tried her weight on it. He held her hand for support. "It will be all right."

"How long were you locked up here?"

"About an hour. You must remember to tell her—"

"An hour! Good God! I'm telling her the truth. This is ridiculous, locking you in attics, as though you were an unruly child, and threatening to whip you."

"Us," she corrected. "You are for the thorn stick, too, for allowing me to behave so badly." She related at more length the story she had told Lady Healy.

"We're marching straight down there and telling her the truth," he said, lifting his chin in a determined way. Then he looked about him, gradually realizing that he was not able to do anything of the sort. "As soon as I figure out how we are to get down from here," he added.

"Now don't be rash, Whewett. We have been through too much to throw it all to the winds now. Think of Augusta's fortune."

"To hell with Augusta's fortune. We don't need the money. It is a luxury. How *dare* she treat you like this! As though you were a—"

"Yes, but so far as she knows, I *am* a child. She hasn't an inkling of the truth. It will only be for another day or so. Is Daugherty going to buy the estate?"

"Yes, it will take him a day to get the cash assembled, and meanwhile we'll have the mortgage papers drawn up."

"Well then, we can stick it for one more day."

Whewett smiled a rueful smile, shaking his head. "I'm damnably sorry about this, Grace. What an unconscionable way I have treated you. Allowed her to treat you, I mean. I feel wretched about it. I'll make it up to you," he promised, placing his hands on her wrists.

"The price has been agreed upon. I am not a rack-rent."

"The initial offer did not include incarceration in a stifling attic and threats of violence."

"Or starvation," she added wanly.

"She didn't feed you?" he demanded with a kindling eye.

"Not a bite, and I am likewise to be robbed of dinner. But she's only pretending to be angry. She wanted to laugh."

"You shall have dinner and luncheon. You are my daughter! She has no right—"

"Better make sure she means to let you have a crumb before you start making threats. I must advise you, Whewett, you are in even deeper disgrace than myself."

"How could she believe me so foolish as to let my daughter carry on like that?" he asked, hardly able to credit it.

"She found that easier to credit than that you had a lightskirt stashed away. I guess she hasn't heard about Doll. But you are only my dupe, you know. I always could wind you round my thumb."

He squeezed her fingers. "Poor Gussie."

"It wasn't so bad. I knew she wouldn't really hurt me."

"I didn't mean you. I meant my daughter. She would no more pull off a stunt like this than she'd grow fins and take to the deep blue seas."

"But you cannot throw away her rightful inheritance. You must swallow your pride and see this through. And you must stick up for me, too. I am really very hungry, Whewett."

He accepted her advice and was struck most forcibly by her courage and tenacity, especially as her own reward was so trifling. "Not to worry. You are ill—prostrated from the heat in this oven. I shall enforce my rights as your father."

Grace congratulated him with a pert smile. "That's a good boy, Papa." Even as he looked, her smile faded. He followed the line of her glance and saw the butler sticking his head out the window.

"Can I help yez, milord?" the man asked, displaying none of the curiosity he must surely be feeling.

"Yes, will you toss us out a ladder, please."

"I'll have to go to the shed and fetch it."

"Do it, then," Whewett said in an impatient voice not normally used to servants. The head disappeared.

"It's not his fault," Grace pointed out.

"I know perfectly well whose fault it is. I *said* I'm sorry," he answered rather sharply. He shook his head, running his fingers along the furrows of his brow. "I *am* sorry, Grace."

"Oh, stop apologizing," she scolded.

"You don't seem to realize the position I have placed you in. Townsend's mother is now broadcasting your name the length and breadth of the country as my—whatever," he finished with an ambiguous flutter of his hand.

"Mistress," she replied grimly.

"Something of the sort."

"I do regret that."

Instead of trying to reassure her, Whewett went on to paint a bleak picture. "She will have discovered by now that Miss Farnsworth is no kin to my wife. She will discover you do not reside at Tunbridge Wells and jump to the conclusion her sort always leap to. She'll think we met there for some obscene carrying on."

"You don't have to draw me a picture, Whewett. I know what she will think—and say—to anyone who will listen."

"This was a wretched idea I had, bringing you here."

"You did not force me. I came of my own will. It is not as though I am some famous debutante who ever expected to make a grand match. I doubt if this *on dit* will cause a ripple in the saloons of London. It is just that a governess must have a sterling reputation—oh, why are we being so pessimistic? We shall figure out something," she said, but her pale, worried face told him she was more disturbed than she admitted.

"I have already thought of something. Marriage," he said in a businesslike way. "I have compromised your good name and am ready to do the proper thing."

Marriage! The word caught her unawares. She had expected another offer of increasing her salary. Being only human, Grace had given a thought to what it would be like to be Whewett's wife. She could not think of a more appealing husband, but to win him by such a shady means—no, never. "That is a gentlemanly offer but unnecessary," she replied, with an enigmatic little smile.

"I hope I am a gentleman and behave like one—when I am not behaving like a jackass."

"You have always behaved like a gentleman with me, and I do not mean to take advantage of you."

"We could visit a bishop, get a special license, and be married the very day Grandma leaves."

169

He meant it! Temptation tugged at her heart, but Grace was a lady as surely as Whewett was a gentleman, and could not press her advantage over him. "We are not ready for such desperate measures as marriage," she said firmly. "I don't know anyone in Tunbridge Wells except Miss Thomas, and she is aware of the truth. Let your cousin do her worst. It will be only a nine days' wonder, if that."

This settled, Grace walked off to peep over the edge of the roof, pointing out the unusual view. Whewett strolled after her, so preoccupied he did not even think to utter any words of caution, but when she leaned over too far to please him, he took her hand and pulled her silently back.

Chapter Fifteen

Lord Whewett and Lady Healy exchanged many a silent, fierce scowl while the terms of the sale to Daugherty were hammered out. As soon as the buyer and his agent left, he turned on her. "I have already told you my daughter's health is delicate, madam. She has collapsed from the heat in the attic. You must allow *me* to decide what is best for her in future, or I shall remove her at once."

"Collapsed, that sturdy girl? Nothing of the sort. She was shamming it," she insisted mulishly, but her next speech showed her concern. "Is she really ill, Alfred? Should I call in a sawbones for her?"

"That won't be necessary, but she must certainly have her meals."

"What is amiss with her? Does she take these spells often?"

"No. She has been improving in recent months."

"I'll have Mulkins take her up some lemonade."

"And sandwiches. She is starving."

Mulkins was called and told to take Lady Augusta up refreshments.

"It is growing pains that make her feel peaky," was the dame's next speech. "You have not noticed, but your daughter is growing up on you. Breasts, Whewett. She has started growing breasts."

"I have noticed," he said curtly.

"That girl is going to be a holy terror when she gets going. I remember very well borrowing Mama's slippers and long gowns when I was young, but I must say my papa did not encourage me in this vice."

"If Gussie wishes to cut up a lark, it is better for her to do it when I am there to protect her," he pointed out reasonably.

"There is a grain of sense in that and a peck of nonsense. It makes her think you approve. They will always go a pace beyond what their parents approve, you must know. That is the whole point of being young."

"We have a better understanding than that."

"What a sweet child it is. Not one of those mealy-mouthed gels, as I feared any daughter of yours and Irene's must be. She has life. What a complexion—with just a touch of bran on her nose. You must buy her a parasol."

He looked at Lady Healy, whose face and hands were bedizened with brown age spots. "Don't judge by what you see now," she said angrily. "I was prettier than Augusta in my day, though she takes after me in spirits. I wish I had known the truth when Mrs. Townsend was here, and I would have put a flea in her ear. 'A saucy piece of merchandise' she had the nerve to call her. She will traduce Miss Farnsworth up and down the land. What a trick to

172

play on the poor governess. I daresay it is no more than the woman deserves, if the truth were known."

"You are mistaken. Miss Farnsworth is unexceptionable."

"Perhaps. Now about Daugherty—tomorrow the deal will be closed. Saturday. We cannot desecrate the Sabbath with travel. We shall leave and go our separate ways on Monday, bright and early. About Augusta's trip to Scotland—"

Whewett had decided that the attic episode would serve as an excuse to forbid the trip. No excuse was necessary. "I am going to delay the visit a little," she said. "She will be disappointed, for we both looked forward to it. The truth is, her high spirits are too much for me to cope with till I have recovered from this journey. When I feel more stout, I shall send for her. Invers can accompany her north—I quite depend on her common sense. It is all I *can* depend on, for it is clear *you* have no control over the chit, buying her bonnets that are fitter for the muslin company."

Weak with relief, Whewett put up little fight. "It is an excellent bonnet. I selected it myself."

"I suspected as much. That high poke must have looked like a stove pipe on her little head. I shall have her model it for me before we leave. And soon you will send her to me. No excuses, now."

He felt fairly confident that the event would never occur. Lady Healy herself probably knew it but refused to face the truth. "Write and let us know when you are feeling more the thing," he said.

"It will be sooner than you think," she warned, having jumped to the conclusion that he was patronizing her.

"I hope so."

"Humph. You must exercise a more proper regard for your daughter's behavior in future. Call Mulkins. I am shaken to pieces with having to scold Augusta. She knows I didn't mean it," she added in an uncharacteristically mild way.

"Of course she does. I am going up to her now."

"Tell her I shall be up to her later."

Whewett went abovestairs. Daylight lent some aura of propriety to his being in Grace's room. Her outfit, too, was that of a juvenile. It was only her lounging at ease on the bed that lent any air of depravity to the visit. "Are we for whipping at the cart's tail or the dungeon?" she asked, sitting up.

"Neither one. There is good news and bad. The bad news is that we are here till Monday. I must stay for the closing of the deal tomorrow, to make sure Bronfman does not hoodwink Grandmama on the mortgage."

"We could leave as soon as it is signed."

"Not much point leaving late in the afternoon."

"Sunday morning, then."

"Desecrate the Sabbath by sitting at ease in a carriage? Did you learn nothing from all that Bible reading? Besides, we have not decided where you are to be taken."

"I shall go to Miss Thomas."

"To Tunbridge Wells, where Miss Farnsworth's reputation is the talk of the town?" Whewett saw the indecision on her face and braced himself for a different suggestion. "You shall come to Downsfield with me, as soon as I come up with a chaperon." He saw no signs of outrage but only surprise.

"No, that is not at all sensible."

174

"The Townsend business changes everything. You must see that," he said reasonably.

It had indeed made Tunbridge Wells ineligible, and Grace had no other spot to suggest. "Is London very far?" she asked. It seemed big enough to become lost in.

"Not too far. I have several relatives in London. We'll go there and talk some maiden aunt into coming to Dover with us. In fact ..." He stopped, to think out the details.

"Yes?"

Whewett felt uncertain of his ground, and to remove any aura of embarrassment, he spoke in a brusque manner. "It might be a good idea to be married there. In that way we can dispose of the maiden aunt. They can be the very devil to root out, once they're installed."

Grace noticed that his talk of marriage had no tinge of romance. It was conducted along strictly business lines. "It might be a good idea *if* we were planning to be married. I, for one, am not. Now, let us talk sense, if you please."

"If it is common sense you're looking for, marriage is the answer. You need a position; I need a wife; Gussie needs a mother. It is the sensible, convenient course."

He looked at her closely, trying to read her reaction. A smile at the corner of her lips led him to believe she found the idea attractive. As it stretched into a grin, however, he realized that whatever in his plan amused her, it was not what pleased himself. "Here I thought you were turning into a foolish romantic on me, Whewett. Gentlemen do at forty or so, you recall. You are too young for me."

175

He studied her with a sapient eye. "Too *old* for you is what you mean."

"I am too young for you. It amounts to the same thing. I am not really ready to settle for a sensible marriage of convenience. My mind has disintegrated from too long a perusal of *Pamela*. I insist on a happy, romantic ending." She waited, wondering if he would follow up this lead . . . wishing.

He listened, not trusting himself to speak for a moment. "I understand," he said curtly, and then turned to look out the window for a moment. He was a fool to think Grace was interested in him. What would that vibrant, fun-loving, lively girl want with his aging self? When he looked back, he seemed to have forgotten all about marriage. "We shall leave early Monday for London. You can stay with one of my relatives till Mary returns. If she does not require a governess, my aunts will see you are well placed. They have a wide circle of friends and acquaintances. About your payment for this acting chore, Grace, the original sum is so small in light of all the hardships you have been subjected to that it amounts to a joke. I shall have a thousand pounds made over to you, if that is satisfactory."

"I thought perhaps—two hundred," she countered.

"A thousand. I have told Lady Healy you are not feeling well. Mulkins is making some lunch, and Lady Healy will drop in later. It would help if you could act invalidish."

"Heat prostration calls for plenty of liquids. Wine would do nicely," she said, trying for a light air.

"There was a mention of lemonade. Can I get you anything else—books, cards? Nothing is too good for my invalid daughter," he added with a show of good humor he was far from feeling.

"A smile?" she suggested in a coaxing way.

"You ask too much. Rejected gentlemen are not expected to receive their refusal with a smile." He gazed at her a moment, examining her as if for the last time. "But for you I shall make the effort," he said in an uneven voice.

The effort was not successful. There was much of regret in it. His eyes lingered longer than was comfortable. For one wild moment Grace felt it possible that the offer had been made from the heart. But he had said, in so many words, it would be sensible and convenient and that Augusta needed a mother. The word love had not arisen. He felt sorry for her, that was all.

"I'll try to hurry Mulkins up," he said. Then he bowed and turned to leave.

"Whowott!" she called, for no reason but that she did not want him to leave. He looked over his shoulder, and she remembered something to ask him. "You said there was good news and bad. What was the good news? Was it that you would marry me?"

"That was not good news to you apparently. Neither was it what I meant. One item of some importance slipped my mind. Grandma has postponed your visit north. She is not up to entertaining a rambunctious youngster, poor old girl. The visit will never come. If she raises it at some future time, I'll find an excuse."

"That's a relief."

"Yes." He left then.

Grace lay on the counterpane and puzzled over the visit. She had been so flustered at his proposal that she had forgotten all about going to Scotland.

She knew he was serious about marrying her. Whewett would not joke about such a thing and would perhaps even take some pleasure from having her at Downsfield. But it was not the pleasure normally associated with marriage that he wanted. It was not the same pleasure that she wanted. The most contrary thing of all was that if she had not stupidly gone falling in love with Whewett, she would marry him in a flash. So kind, so gentlemanly and considerate, yet not without humor and a sense of adventure. He would have been an ideal employer, but that was no longer enough. A week's masquerade had shown her it was not a career she could undertake for life.

And if she married him, they would go on much as they had been doing, like father and daughter, or perhaps eventually brother and sister. No, it would never do. Perhaps once they were at Downsfield, constantly together, she could slowly insinuate herself into his heart. She would turn the conversation back to the subject when he brought her lunch.

Grace put on her brightest smile when the expected tap was heard on the door a few moments later, but it was only a servant holding her tray. Whewett would bring her a book or some cards—he was waiting till she had eaten, that's all. Lady Healy came and sat for half an hour, first jawing about her "shameless spree," then discussing the delayed visit. She returned again in the evening, and still Whewett had not been back.

When Lady Healy claimed she was as tired, as if she had been hunting all day and went to her bed, Grace decided to give Whewett a little surprise when he came to say good night. She would appear

178

as an adult. She hastily changed into her own suit and arranged her coiffure as attractively as she could. The face staring back at her from her dim mirror was undeniably that of a fully mature lady, and a lady ready to do battle for what she wanted. Her chin was lifted high, her eyes sparkling, and her color brightened with excitement.

She heard him enter his room and flew from the mirror, like an assassin from the scene of his crime. He paced to and fro, talking to someone. That was why he delayed coming to her. Who could it be? An ear to the door told her it was only his valet. The voices stopped, and Grace hurried from the door, but still the expected tap did not come. When at last it was heard, Whewett did no more than peep his head in through the partially open door.

"Is everything all right?" he asked.

Peeved with her long vigil, she answered sharply, "No, it is not all right. I have never had such a boring day in my life."

"There is no need to stay cooped up tomorrow. Lady Healy and I will be busy all afternoon with Daugherty and Bronfman. You can go for a walk, or take a spin on the nag I hired from the inn. But don't go into Wickfield. Why are you wearing that outfit?" he asked at last. It had taken him that long even to notice and that further goaded Grace.

"I am tired with being a child."

"It won't be for much longer. Why don't you go to bed now? It's been a tiring day."

"Aren't you going to come in and talk to me? I've hardly seen a soul all day."

"I'm in my dressing gown. I'm ready for bed," he replied. "It is hardly an appropriate way to visit a lady."

179

"You might have thought of that before you undressed."

There was no misreading that long indrawn sigh. It revealed boredom, just verging on impatience. "Is there something in particular you wish to discuss? I can get dressed, if—"

Her pride prevented pushing the matter further. "No, nothing in particular. Nothing I cannot say to myself, or the doll, or the chair. Good night, Whewett. I hope you sleep well."

His fingers began drumming the doorjamb. "What is it? What is bothering you, Grace?"

"Never mind. You will want to get your twelve hours of sleep for the heavy exertion of watching Lady Healy sign the papers tomorrow."

A reluctant smile tugged at his harsh features. "When my daughter becomes cranky and ill-mannered, I turn her over my knee and give her a good whopping. I shall take my leave before I am tempted to do the same to you. Good night."

The door was quietly closed in her face, depriving her of the satisfaction of slamming it. "Don't forget to put on the bolt," she called in a last burst of annoyance.

There was no verbal reply but only the sound of sliding metal, which so inflamed her that she picked up a book and threw it at the closed door. And still he did not say anything.

Chapter Sixteen

Saturday was only slightly less tedious than Friday. Grace visited with Lady Healy, read her Bible and did not see a sign of Whewett till luncheon, when he treated her like a daughter. His conversation with Lady Healy revealed that he had done nothing more important that morning than sort through papers in various desks and drawers, as the house was sold furnished. He could have been with her if he had wanted to. In fact, she could have helped him. He was avoiding her.

When Bronfman and Daugherty came to close the deal in the afternoon, Grace had a ride through the park on Whewett's hired nag. For a full year now she had been wanting to feel a horse under her, and it was strange that it gave her so little pleasure. In the end she cut the ride short, to be at the house as soon as the deal was closed. As Whewett had nothing else to do, he would be forced to spend some time with her, for civility's sake.

He was sitting with Grandma in the Purple Saloon, which seemed as gloomy as a dungeon after her ride in the sunlight. "Augusta shall have a glass of wine with us to celebrate the sale," Lady Healy decreed. "I wish I had seen you ride, Gussie. Keep your back straight but not stiff. Neither a reed nor a ramrod is wanted in the saddle. I was a famous horsewoman in my day. Most wild youngsters want to run away and be an actress." Grace glanced at Whewett, but he was looking out the window. "For me it was Astley's Circus. It was a great letdown when I finally saw it. I could have done better than any of them."

Grace sipped the wine, hiding her sulks to please the old lady. "We shall find a good mount for you when you come to Scotland," Lady Healy continued. "And I shall enroll you in the Hunt, too. They shan't see my five thousand if they don't accept you." She chattered on, monopolizing the conversation with no trouble, as the others found little to say.

Grace glanced at the mantel clock and looked hopefully at Whewett. There was time for a walk, if he would only drink up his wine. He reached out and filled his glass again. There was to be no privacy, then, no return to the subject of marriage. Grace was too disappointed to be very angry.

Lady Healy was hitting her stride in tales of the Hunt when the door knocker sounded. "Who can that be?" she scolded. "I did not advertise I was here. I want to remember my friends as they were, not see them sunk to old relicts like myself."

The groom-butler sauntered to the door and said, "There's a woman here says she's Lady Dewitt."

Grace's face turned white, and she turned a wild

eye to Whewett, who looked much the way she felt. A pretty young matron dressed in the highest kick of fashion came prancing in, followed by a shy, pale young girl.

Lady Healy cast an offended frown on the interloper. "Who, pray tell, is Lady Dewitt?" she demanded. "Is she one of your women, Whewett?"

The matron threw her head back and laughed in sheer astonishment. "Oho, you have changed, Alfred!" she said, shaking a finger at him.

"This is my sister, Mary," Whewett said in a strangled voice. He looked quite simply bewildered as his eyes darted in hopeless confusion from Lady Dewitt to the young girl, to Grace, and lastly to Lady Healy. Lady Dewitt performed a graceful curtsy.

"Eh? I thought she lived in Ireland," Lady Healy said. "Well, I'm very happy to make your acquaintance, Lady Dewitt. Is this your gel? Sickly looking creature. She wants fresh air and exercise."

Lady Dewitt raised her brows in her brother's direction and replied, "Why no, this is Whewett's daughter, ma'am. Say hello to your papa, my dear."

The pale girl gave one frightened look at Lady Healy before running forward to throw herself into Whewett's arms. She burrowed her head into his shoulder as though to escape the frightening old lady. His arms went around her protectively, tightening when Lady Healy rose to her feet in wrath. She clutched her blackthorn stick menacingly. Her lined face had turned an alarming shade of purple. "What—is—the—meaning—of—this!" she demanded in an awful voice.

Lady Dewitt stared, more fascinated than frightened at the spectacle she was witnessing. Grace felt as if she were in a nightmare. Her worst fear had come true. She was about to be revealed in all her tawdry shame, not only to Lady Healy, but to Whewett's elegant sister and his daughter. Her eyes turned beseechingly to Whewett.

He kept his composure better than she dared to hope. "You heard the lady," he said, addressing himself to Lady Healy. "This is my daughter. Make a curtsy to your grandmother, my dear." He detached Augusta's arms from around his neck.

Augusta, wide-eyed and trembling, made a brief, awkward curtsy, before returning to hold on to her father for dear life.

Grace sat numb with apprehension, waiting for the blow to fall. On top of everything else she felt in her bones that Lady Dewitt was not at all the sort of employer she wanted or who would want her. She had imagined Mary as a pleasant, comfortable lady, rather like Whewett. What the outcome of it all would be she could not even imagine, but the blackthorn across her back certainly featured in it. She was every bit as apprehensive as poor Gussie, cowering against her father. Whewett had been correct not to bring the child here.

"You ought to be ashamed of yourself," Lady Healy ranted. The brunt of her wrath was directed at Whewett. "Bringing your by-blow into a decent house, scandalizing your own daughter—*and me*! And *you*, I take leave to tell you, Lady Dewitt, have no more sense than a peagoose. Come with me, Augusta. When we return, we shall expect to find the saloon empty. Good day."

"What is going on here?" Lady Dewitt asked in hopeless dismay. "Alfred—" She looked to him. He hunched his shoulders behind Lady Healy's back and tossed up his hands.

Lady Healy strode to Grace, grabbed her hand, and sailed from the room without another glance at such disreputable connections as sullied her saloon. Grace, hobbling along beside her, had time for only one brief glimpse of the scene she left behind. She saw the brother and sister trying to contain their explosions of nervous laughter till the old lady was beyond hearing.

"Alfred, I hope you have an explanation for this," Lady Dewitt said. She sank onto a sofa.

"What the devil possessed you to come here?" he demanded.

"Why, when we heard at Downsfield where you had gone and why, I made sure you would want Gussie to meet her grandma. I was put to considerable trouble with the extra trip. Who was the young girl with Lady Healy?"

"She called her Augusta, the same name as me," Gussie said, reviving now that the termagent with the black eyes was gone.

"Ahem, it will be best if I explain it to you later, Sis," Whewett said, shooting a warning glance to Gussie. Then he turned his attention to his daughter. "How is my girl?"

"Fine. I had a wonderful visit, Papa. But who was that girl with grandma? What did she mean about you scandalizing me?"

Lady Dewitt said, "Alfred, you cannot mean to tell me that young girl is really your—" She stopped, with a quick look at her niece.

"I'll take you to the inn," Whewett decided, arising to call his carriage. "We can talk there."

"Our carriage is just outside, and we are already

booked at the inn. Invers is there now, unpacking. When we heard in the village that Willowcrest had been sold, we feared the place would be in an upheaval. I must say, we did not anticipate such a hot reception!"

Any discussion was impossible on the trip to the inn, as Whewett took his own carriage, to facilitate his return. Until Augusta had been handed over to Invers at the inn, she and her father discussed the visit to Ireland. The instant Invers took Augusta away, Lady Dewitt said, "I have never been so curious in my life, Alfred. Do tell me all about it. Is that girl your daughter? I know she is, for she looks very much like Doll. Why did you never tell me? Where have you kept her all this time, and what in the world possessed you to take her to Lady Healy, of all people?"

"She's not my daughter! I never saw her in my life till the day I came here," he began. "I hired her to act as my daughter. Grandma would be in the boughs that Gussie had gone off to Ireland, when I always claimed she was delicate."

"What have the girl's parents to say about it?"

"She has none living. She's a governess."

"At thirteen or so years of age? Now do cut line, Alfred."

"She's, er, a little older than that. She is small you see, short."

"How much older?" Mary asked, her eyes brightly quizzical.

"She's twenty-two. I know it was a hare-brained scheme, but we had no idea how the thing would drag out," he began, and explained how the visit had grown and some of the difficulties met along the way. "Now that Gussie is here, I hardly know

186

what to do. We are not to leave till Monday. Gussie is petrified of Lady Healy, and the old lady has no opinion of her, either. Gussie does look pale. Has she been ill?"

"Just fatigued from traveling. I am worn to a thread myself."

"Grandma would come to love her if there were time, but there isn't. Meanwhile she has become so fond of the stand-in that it would upset her dreadfully to learn the trick we played. Her heart is not sound. Really, I don't think I can risk telling her the truth."

Lady Dewitt was still confused. "I cannot think how you came to do such a thing, Alfred. It is so shabby—and daring. It is not like you."

"I meant no harm. I believe I must just let Grandma think me a lecher, with a by-blow hidden away all these years. She won't really mind that, you know, once she gets used to the idea."

"She minded very much! If she hadn't needed that stick to prop herself up, she would have laid it over someone's back."

"She minded having what she believed to be an illegitimate child in her saloon without her permission. That is why you were castigated as a peagoose, for having brought her. Manners concern her somewhat more than morality, though she would stare to hear me say so. She likes to think herself holy, now that she approaches the end. I don't mean to sound hard on her. She's a great old lady. I hardly know what to do. I won't draw Gussie into posing as my illegitimate daughter—not any further, I mean. Gussie must be left out of it."

"Once her shock has subsided, Lady Healy may want to see your by-blow."

"She *has* seen her, or thinks she has. Any illegitimate child of mine would be of little interest to her, having no Brougham blood in her. Grandma does not relish much excitement in her poor condition. I shall say my rag-mannered sister left the neighborhood and took the child with her somewhere or other."

"Would it help if we let on the child lived with me?"

"It might do—give her the idea that her granddaughter is not exposed to such depravity. Can you and Invers and Gussie stay here till Monday, and we'll all leave in a caravan for Downsfield?"

"Surely. We are in sore need of a rest. What will become of the governess? Miss Farnsworth, did you say the name is?"

"Grace Farnsworth. She is a very nice girl, Mary, from a good family. Don't judge her by this first impression. She only did it as a favor to me and because she was in desperate need of money."

Mary regarded him with a wary eye. "But what is to become of her, Alfred?"

"I had planned to take her to London to find a position—if you do not require the services of a very capable young lady, that is to say. I admit, the first thing that popped into my head was to send her to you. You would like her. So lively and vivacious. I cannot begin to tell you all the adventures we have had. She's very pretty, too, when she is not dressed as a child."

"Prettiness is not one of my requisites in a governess, Alfred," she said. Her suspicions rose higher at every speech. "Nor anyone else's, either. Quite the contrary. Unless the employer happens to be a *widower*, of course."

188

"There is nothing like that between us," he said swiftly. No one but a sister would have detected the trace of pink around his ears, the quickly averted eye, the nonchalant toss of the head.

Lady Dewitt, as sharp-eyed as a lynx, certainly noticed it, and wondered whether Alfred was not being conned by a sly wench. "Would she be willing to leave you, to accompany me to Ireland?" she asked.

"She would be very happy to. We have spoken of it."

"Good. I am vastly relieved to hear you have not spoken of marrying her instead. It would be just like you, to be taken in by a cunning mushroom."

"Grace is not cunning!" he said angrily. "She has not been throwing her bonnet at me, if that is what your sniff implies."

"I don't suppose she would say no if you offered."

"You are mistaken. She did say no," Whewett answered before realizing he was being led down the garden path.

"I see! I like her better already. She has given you a chance to cry off if you are only offering from a sense of duty. As it happens, dear Alfred, I *do* require a governess," she told him, depending on his perseverance with Miss Farnsworth that she would not end up with two, for she had an unexceptionable one already, older and ugly, just as she liked.

"But you said you did not," he objected.

"My present one is poor at French, and it is time to start the girls on it. Does Miss Farnsworth speak French?"

"Yes, but—" Invention failed him, and he was forced to simulate pleasure at Grace's good fortune.

189

His sister was too shrewd to be taken in by such lukewarm assertions as "That is excellent news."

"Of course I shall want to become acquainted with Miss Farnsworth before I engage her," Mary said. "Can she come to Downsfield with us?"

"She will be happy to," he said eagerly.

"If we two rub along satisfactorily during my visit, she shall return with me. And if she does not appeal to me, I daresay you will think of a different role for her. But I warn you, Alfred, I cannot stay longer than a week."

Whewett missed the laughing gleam in her eye. "Stay longer, Mary," he urged. "A month—"

"It took *you* less than a week to discover her excellent qualities. I am not slower than you."

With the important matter of an immediate destination in mind, they talked of other matters. Later Whewett went to see his daughter before turning his carriage back to Willowcrest.

Grace awaited him in the Purple Saloon. A smile was the last expression she expected to see on him. Her own face was white and drawn with anxiety. She looked like a little wraith in the surrounding gloom of that ghastly chamber. "She's ready to kill you, Whewett," she warned him. "I have been put through such a catechism! She thinks Augusta is illegitimate and has asked me a *million* questions about her. I claimed to know nothing about it."

"Good. How should you? We have decided she has been making her home in Ireland with Mary. You have never been there."

"Are we not going to tell her the truth, then? I must caution you, she has taken the real Augusta in the greatest dislike. It was a wretched thing we did. We might lose Augusta's fortune for her, and it is only the circumstances that have set Grandma's jaw against her."

"Everything is fine," Whewett said airily.

"I don't know how you can say so. It could hardly be worse. I am strongly inclined to sneak out the door while I have my hide in one piece."

"We'll let her believe me a libertine and a scoundrel. It will not affect Gussie's inheritance. We shall carry on as we've been doing till Monday, if you are willing; then we all go to Downsfield. Mary wants you for a governess."

Grace looked at him, unable to believe it. "How can she possibly, after meeting me for the first time under such abominable circumstances? She must think me the greatest wretch who ever drew breath."

"I explained everything. She is eager to engage you."

"What did you tell her?"

"Only the good things. I withheld all references to the stage, marrying aged widowers, that avidity for food and wine. It is all settled but for you to agree. You will come, won't you?" he asked eagerly.

"Yes, I suppose, But first I must meet Mary—Lady Dewitt—under more regular circumstances and see how we go along together. I own it would be a great relief to have somewhere decent to go. Have you ever been to Ireland, Whewett?"

"I've visited Mary a few times. It's lovely. You will be happy there, and I shall know where to find you, should I require a spare daughter for some rig or other," he added, smiling. It was not precisely a happy smile. There was some wistful quality to it.

"I couldn't go through with it again."

"We'll keep in touch, Grace. Now I must go upstairs and face the wrath of Lady Jehovah. A regular dirge it will be, if I know anything."

"A very lively, angry dirge. If you are wise, you will take a poker to defend yourself. She has been threatening to lay that cane across your shoulders."

"The wages of sin," he said with a shrug, and went up to confront Lady Healy.

The sound of the old lady's voice raised very high was soon echoing down the staircase, with some intervening silences to indicate that Whewett occasionally got a word in edgewise. He heard he was an unconscionable dastard, a perpetrator of lewd behavior, not worthy to wipe Irene's boots, and if the silly chit had used her wits, she would not have made such an appalling match in the first place.

Enjoying her rant to the hilt, Lady Healy went on to describe his bastard as a whey-faced moonling, and a demmed ugly one to boot. His sister was no better than she should be to let the bastard under her roof to corrupt her own children, and Irene was a knock-in-the-cradle ever to have given him the time of day. He took it like a rock, and after her wrath was spent, Whewett also heard that Lady Healy was too fair-minded to deprive Augusta of her fortune only because her father's carrying on was enough to shame the nation. At the end he also heard he had given his hostess such a setback, she was unable to leave her chamber, and he must dine alone. She was in such a state, she forgot to give any orders regarding Augusta, so that, in fact, Whewett dined with his alleged daughter and enjoyed a happier meal than he had partaken of under that roof since his arrival.

"Still in one piece?" Grace asked when he descended.

"Bloody but unbowed. She combed my hair with the footstool. Had herself a marvelous time but never once threatened to change the will. I'm amazed. Something else amazes me, too," he added with a quizzing smile.

"What is that?"

"It is half an hour past dinner time, and you haven't mentioned food."

"I haven't even thought of it," she said, and was surprised herself.

After dinner Grace played the pianoforte for Whewett. She thought he would take advantage of the privacy to speak again of marriage, but he seemed happy to just watch her and listen. After playing for some time, Grace joined him.

"I hope you will play for me when we go home," he said. "My piano at Downsfield is not so badly out of tune, for Invers gives Gussie lessons."

He rose at once and said, "How quickly the evening has flown. You will want to get some rest after this taxing day. I have a little accounting to do before I retire, so I shall say good-night now, Grace."

"Good night, Whewett," she said rather cooly, and went upstairs, realizing that she would not see him again that night.

Chapter Seventeen

Lady Healy came to the table on Sunday morning, but to show her disapproval of Whewett, she said not a word to him. She gave many instructions to his daughter, finishing with the warning that as Lord Whewett had no interest in his daughter's welfare, she must pay close heed to her grandmother. "Always remember you have good Brougham blood in your veins as well as that other bad stuff."

When the meal was over, Lady Healy had to bend her vow not to speak to Whewett. "You will no doubt go into the village to visit your sister and your bastard. Augusta will not accompany you. As I notice you are not in the habit of taking her to church on Sunday, she shall read her Bible." On this speech she clomped out of the room, leaning heavily on her cane.

The minute she was gone, Whewett said to Grace, "My Gussie will wonder why you are not with me.

She is eager to meet you." Yet, for the first time in years, there was someone he would rather be with than his daughter. "Lady Healy has hinted I may remain away for lunch. I shall return for dinner, giving her one last chance to have at me. Take care, Grace."

The day dragged by slowly, with nothing of much interest occurring at Willowcrest. Grace rode and read without taking much pleasure from either. By evening Lady Healy's curiosity about the illegitimate child, and more precisely the child's mother, had reached such heights that she gave over being silent with Whewett and returned to the attack.

"Who was the hussy, eh? Some tavern wench, I warrant, from the looks of the parcel she foisted on you."

"You would not be interested. You don't know the lady."

"I *am* interested, I tell you. I would not ask if I weren't. When did it happen? Was it while you were married to Irene?"

"Certainly not."

"The child is younger than Augusta. I ain't blind. She was born a good year or more after your legal daughter. It was while Irene was enceinte. You men always think that a good enough excuse to set up a convenient. If I had had the least notion you was a rake, Whewett, you would not have married my granddaughter, and so I tell you."

"Many times now, Lady Healy."

"You're shameless. A disgrace and a scandal. Who was she?"

"A lady, a widow," he said, hoping to satisfy her.

"Lady, hah! Lady's maid at best. I expect you are still running after the low-born wenches if the truth were known. For the sake of your immortal soul, you had best take a wife if you cannot control your base impulses. I hope He may forgive you for all the other women you have ruined in the meanwhile."

Whewett stolidly cut his meat and ate it. "Now, who shall you marry?" was her next question, which she went on to consider quite independently of the groom's wishes. "Not that Elton creature, with her straw hair and painted face. It would not be necessary to marry the likes of her to have your way with her. Fondling her in conservatories! We shall be fortunate if you haven't ruined your child's morals as well as your own."

"Discussing it in front of her won't help," he said.

"Let her find out what men are like. Here is what passes for a *good* man in the world, Augusta. You may imagine what the bad ones are up to. You shall marry Lady Eleanor, Whewett."

"I am afraid not, ma'am."

"Not wanton enough for you? The governess, then. You say she can handle him, Augusta?"

Grace had all the lively embarrassment of commenting on herself. "Pretty well, Grandma," she said.

"Is she a decent sort of woman?"

"Oh, yes—that is, fairly decent," she added in confusion.

"That is, as decent as your father could endure. What of her looks? We don't want any more of those demmed whey-faced brats running around the world calling Whewett Papa." She turned to Whewett before Grace was required to describe her appearance. "Make her an offer when you get home.

196

I want to receive a wedding notice in the near future."

Whewett leveled a cool stare across the table at Grace. She lowered her eyes to avoid looking at him. "I have already offered for her. She refused."

"That shows she has some taste," Lady Healy said. "Get rid of those tavern wenches who are giving her a disgust of you, and ask her again. A penniless governess won't have as good an offer, from a material point of view. There, it is settled. I am going to bed. We arise at seven. Come and kiss me good-night, Augusta." Grace did as she was told. Whewett received an angry scowl and a sound that might have meant good night, and Lady Healy was gone.

"Thank God that is over," he said, looking after her departing form. "I keep thinking how disastrous it would have been had Gussie gone to Scotland and been subjected to one of her rages. Gussie is so petrified of her that she does not want to go on writing to her."

"You must write the letters in her name."

"I'll work something out. It is a detail."

"It will be important to Grandma. Will you tell Augusta the truth about all this one day?"

"Perhaps, when she is old enough to understand. Well, our adventure is about over, Grace. You have been a formidable ally. How do I thank you?"

"With a check—and of course by helping me conceal my blemishes from your sister till I am safely hired."

"I think this calls for a toast."

"We aren't home free yet," she warned.

"There won't be time in the morning." He filled

197

their glasses, lifted his, and said, "To Miss Farnsworth."

She raised hers. "To Lord Whewett and all his daughters. Or should we say *women*?" she added with an arch smile.

"I'll drink to that. I haven't been having as merry a time as she thinks, you know."

After they had drunk, Grace asked if he knew where Grandma had hidden the pink bonnet and her old slippers.

"I slipped them out to my carriage. You will have to leave here dressed as a child. The best thing will be to change in Mary's room before we leave the inn."

"That will be confusing for Augusta. What will she think?"

"I don't know, but she is not a humorless, spineless child, if that is what you are thinking. She was tired, and frightened of Lady Healy. She likes a good romp as well as anyone. You two will get along famously when you come to know one another," he said, in a considering way, as though thinking aloud.

"I hope so," Grace murmured in much the same spirit.

The last adieus were being said. Lady Healy's antique traveling carriage was pulled up to the door with her trunks tied on top, while Whewett and Grace walked to the road to bid her farewell.

"Don't forget, Augusta, you are to come to me soon. Come in the spring. The Highlands are lovely in spring, with bluebells and heather and all that. You will like it. Till then, be sure to read your Bible and clean your teeth, and take plenty of exercise." She turned to Whewett. "Take good care of her."

"I will," he promised.

The old lady held out her arms for a last embrace from Grace. "You're a fine gel. A fine gel," she said, her voice lowered so Whewett would not hear this weakness.

Grace kissed the lined cheek, feeling the coolness of a tear against her lips. As the final moments drew to a close, Grace felt a wash of regret. She didn't know whether she was glad or sorry she had ever met Lady Healy, but she knew that in some inexplicable way, she would miss the old tyrant. Her own tears, already difficult to control, started to ooze. Soon they were both crying. "I'll miss you, Grandma. I love you. Be sure to write."

"There's a good lass. I'll write often. Take care of your papa. Don't let him run amok with the females. Find him a good wife, you hear?"

"I'll try."

"Good-bye, Whewett." Lady Healy offered her hand. He ignored it and placed a kiss on her cheek. "Flirt! I am too old for you." She laughed, pleased with his gallantry. It was her manner of expressing forgiveness.

"Devil a bit of it." He smiled.

"I am expecting to receive that announcement. A mother for Augusta. Don't disappoint me."

"Before the year is out," he promised rashly.

"About your other daughter," she went on, wanting to apologize without condoning the offense, "she was not so bad. Take care of her, too. It is not the child's fault, after all. Irene would not have begrudged her a decent upbringing. Did Irene know about the girl?"

"No."

"Tell the new wife. Well, I am off. Farewell!"

The door was closed, the horses given the office to begin, and with a great gust of dust from the dry road, the black coach began its long trip to Scotland.

Lady Healy settled comfortably against the squabs and turned to Mulkins with a wise look. "Ha, they think they fooled me with that cock-and-bull story. It was all a sham."

"What do you mean, ma'am" the confused Mulkins asked.

"She is not who they said she is."

"Who, Lady Augusta?"

"Ninnyhammer! Anyone can see Augusta is very like her mama, except that she got something of my spirit. I refer to the female calling herself Lady Dewitt. She was no kin to Whewett. She was his lightskirt. He tried to wrap it up in clean linen, calling her his sister and planning to tell me the gel was Lady Dewitt's daughter, no doubt. But she hadn't the wits to keep her mouth shut. I have been thinking about it and have figured out now why they were all so startled when she came traipsing in with the brat. You saw how Augusta blinked with shock. She didn't recognize the female at all. It was certainly not Lady Dewitt, but Gussie said nothing to give her father away, sly rascal. She thinks the world of him."

"I was not there, milady. I saw nothing," Mulkins said sulkily. Mulkins would have to be buttered up, to restore her to humor after her rough usage at Willowcrest.

"You missed a good show. It was comical to see them all trying to figure out what to say. I enjoyed

200

it immensely. That woman was certainly not Mary. Irene said she was pretty. This one was platter-faced and bold as brass. He will never marry her. She is too forward and common. There was no gallantry in him when he dealt with her. He wanted to wring her neck. I wish he had. Who could she be? She has set her bastard to try to win Whewett for her. Did you see the child hanging on to him?"

"I didn't see anything. I was in the kitchen, ma'am."

"It was famous. I did not think to ask him what he called the brat. I must find out. I shall send her a doll, to show there are no hard feelings. The child was frightened of me. No spirit. Augusta was never frightened of me. I shan't get the bastard a doll with a porcelain head. Not that I begrudge the expense, but it would be sure to get shattered on its way to her."

She settled in and closed her eyes to reminisce about the visit and make plans to keep in touch more closely, but by letter. A visit would be too much exertion, but she was glad she had come. In ten minutes she was snoring.

At Willowcrest Whewett and Grace piled into his carriage and headed to Wickfield, weak with relief that the ordeal was over. Grace was apprehensive regarding her acceptance by Lady Dewitt and how the situation could be explained to Augusta. What never entered her mind, or Whewett's, either, was that Mrs. Sempleton invariably toured the shops on Monday morning to select her greens before the produce was picked over. Busily engaged in talk, they did not observe her as their carriage bolted past, but she saw and recognized them.

Mrs. Sempleton had been able to discover noth-

201

ing of Miss Thomas's whereabouts, but she had learned that her cottage had been let. The child had been seen in the village, so where was she staying? Had Whewett taken her to Willowcrest? This puzzle so intrigued her that she kept an eye on the carriage, and followed it to the inn. A trip to the inn was made plausible by the ruse of buying a journal, which the inn sold at the desk. Thruppence was a stiff price to pay for the information she sought, but she could always just glance at the paper and say it was not the issue she wanted.

This farce proved unnecessary. Mr. Whewett and Miss Jones were still at the desk, inquiring for Lady Dewitt. Mrs. Sempleton had long since discovered this was the elegant female seen on the streets for two days now, accompanied by a young girl who looked too old to be her daughter, yet a trifle young for a sister. The latter relationship had been set upon, however, as the more likely.

"Why, Mr. Whewett!" Mrs. Sempleton said, as though surprised to meet him. "I didn't know you planned to stay so long. I hear the old lady found a taker for Willowcrest. An Irishman, they are saying."

"A Mr. Daugherty, from Kent," he replied with a quizzical glance to Grace, who was trying vainly to disappear into a nearby palm tree.

"And Miss Jones," Mrs. Sempleton continued, twisting her body to get a good look at her. "What on earth are you doing here at the inn with Mr. Whewett?"

Whewett said, "I am giving Miss Jones a drive home to see her baby brother."

"Where have been staying, dear?" the dame

asked. "I know Miss Thomas has left town and have been worried about you."

"I stayed with other friends, ma'am."

She was not let off this easily. "Who would that be, then?"

"With my relatives," Whewett said, taking Grace's arm to lead her off.

Mrs. Sempleton's fingers clutched on to Grace's sleeve, while an eye nearly starting from its socket was turned on Whewett. "What relatives?" she demanded.

"If I thought it would be of the least interest to you, ma'am, I would certainly tell you," he answered pleasantly, then removed her fingers from Grace's arm and walked away, carrying Grace with him.

Within two seconds Mrs. Sempleton had recovered from the shock and said to the clerk, "Call the constable."

The man shook his head. "You'll catch cold at that. That gent is Lord Whewett."

"Yes, and I'm Lady Top o' the Trees. He's plain *Mr.* Whewett is who he is. He's abducting that little girl. He's one of them depraved gentlemen. I know when he did it, too. I am the one let him know she was unprotected. I've as good as thrown the child to the lions. He's been following her about before this. I saw him days ago, dogging her steps down the street. Can you beat that?"

"Mind your own business, Mrs. Sempleton," was the clerk's advice. "Do you want the journal or not?"

She was too excited to answer but not so excited as to lay out thruppence for nothing. She had no real intention of calling a constable. Constables

203

were strangely reluctant to act on her many suggestions. Yet she could not let the matter drop entirely. She loitered in front of the inn, reading coaching timetables with which she was more than familiar, and chatting to passersby. She had a longish wait.

"Wouldn't you know it," Whewett said with a shake of his head as he and Grace hurried upstairs. "I knew we wouldn't get away without that woman spotting us together."

"She didn't believe a word of it!" Grace warned him.

"Nosey old bint. It will keep her busy trying to figure it out. This is Mary's room, " he said, and tapped on the door.

Chapter Eighteen

A less harried perusal of Lady Dewitt showed Grace a pretty, brunette matron in her late twenties. There was a resemblance to Whewett, particularly around the eyes. Those gray eyes were full of mischief at the moment. "I am bursting with curiosity to hear all about it. Did you pull it off?" Lady Dewitt demanded, drawing them into the chamber.

"Do you take us for amateurs, Sis?" Whewett asked, laughing. "Of course we pulled it off. Miss Farnsworth is a famous actress. She speaks of tackling Covent Garden next season."

"Do be serious," Mary chided.

"Where's Gussie?" was his next question.

"I had Invers take her out so we would have some privacy. You mentioned Grace—Miss Farnsworth would want to change her clothes. Charming, Miss Farnsworth," she added, with a smile at the bowed tails of her hair. "You make an excellent child."

"An excellent lady, too," Whewett added.

Lady Dewitt showed Grace into the next room to change into the garments contained in a bandbox. "Where did you find such a good replica of Doll?" she asked her brother when the door was safely closed.

"You noticed it, too. Quite a striking resemblance, particularly when she lets her hair down."

"A telling speech!"

"I mean that literally, Mary. How the deuce did you find out about Doll?"

"It was no secret, dear heart. When the local lord takes up with a dashing article like Dolly, everyone knows about it, even innocent young sisters. It was a scandal. Irene only dead six months, too. We were shocked and horrified you would marry the chit in a fit of lonesomeness or stupidity."

"I wasn't that stupid. I was lonesome, though, and she was a taking little thing, Doll."

"All the gentlemen thought so. Took up with anyone who came along and took anything they offered, too. How could you have been such a clunch, Alfred?"

"You wouldn't understand. I felt half-dead myself when Irene died so young. There seemed no point in anything. Doll was warm and full of fun and alive, and, oh—what's the use? It is ancient history. I never intended to marry her. She was just a woman."

"Mistress, I believe, is the usual term, to differentiate her from the less amusing of us."

"It is as good a word as any. Grace is actually

nothing like her. There is some slight physical resemblance that strikes one at first. It is perhaps
what first attracted me to her—" He stopped sud-
denly, as he realized he was being drawn on to say
more than he intended. "Are you all packed up
and ready to leave?" he asked, to terminate the
subject.

"Not till I squeeze an answer out of you. Is she
decent, Alfred? This whole affair reeks most outra-
geously of impropriety. What, for instance, were the
sleeping arrangements at Willowcrest?"

"Highly unsatisfactory. We had separate rooms.
She is a *lady*, Sis. A very *proper* young lady, who
happened to be in a desperate situation. She still
is."

"Desperate enough to accept the offer you obviously intend making?"

"We shall see. Hush, she's coming."

Grace walked in, transformed into her more mature self. "I don't know what you must think of
me, Lady Dewitt," she said with a beseeching
smile.

"My brother has told me what I am to think,"
Mary answered playfully. Upon receiving a heavy
frown from Whewett, she added, "He tells me you
are a superb governess."

"So she is, but mind, she don't like to get up too
early in the mornings," he said.

"Whewett!" Grace exclaimed, looking to him in
alarm.

"After she has been up all night with the children," he added to his sister.

"I should hope not indeed," Mary said, mystified.
There was an awkward moment's silence, after
which Mary resumed speaking. "I must tell you the

207

story I have told Augusta. I said the girl at Lady Healy's is my governess's younger sister, in case she notices the resemblance. The young sister has gone to relatives far away. Augusta is too young yet to wonder what my governess's sister was doing at Willowcrest."

"So much deception," Grace said unhappily.

"It will not be more than mentioned," Whewett said.

"You will want Gussie in the carriage with you, Alfred," Mary continued, settling the details of their trip. "Shall Miss Farnsworth come with me?"

"No!" he answered without a second's hesitation. "It will be an opportunity for Grace and Gussie to become a little acquainted. Grace will come with us."

Grace looked apologetically to Lady Dewitt, knowing it would make more sense for her to become acquainted with her new employer. She mentioned it, but was quickly overridden.

"You will have plenty of time to know me better at Downsfield before we leave for Ireland," Mary mentioned. "Invers will bear me company on the trip."

They were interrupted by the return of Invers and Augusta. Formal introductions were made. Invers, Grace thought, was rather like her Miss Thomas. She must write dear Thomas a note after she reached Downsfield to tell her the end of the adventure. Lady Augusta was shy, quiet, and very curious. She kept looking at Grace but never ventured from her father's side.

Just before they left, she took a timid step toward Grace. "I am sorry your sister could not come with us to Downsfield, Miss Farnsworth. I hope I can meet her sometime. She looks very much like you, but not quite so pretty."

"Oh, I don't know," Whewett said. "I thought her sister was charming."

"He is teasing, Miss Farnsworth," Augusta explained, blushing for his poor manners. "Papa is a wicked tease."

"Out of the mouths of babes!" Mary laughed. "Shall we be off? I have had the bags stowed on the carriage and settled up the bill earlier to save a few minutes. We can be home by this evening if we get an early start."

They rose to leave. "There is a present for you in the carriage," Whewett told his daughter. "A doll, from your grandmother."

"I thought she hated me! And she was always so nice in her letters."

"She is nice," Whewett said. "She was not feeling well. All the bother of selling Willowcrest, you know. She liked you very much. You would like her, too, if you knew her better."

"I don't want to know her better, Papa. I think she is horrid. She looks like a witch."

Mrs. Sempleton readied herself for action when she espied the party coming out of the inn. As the footman opened the carriage door, she bounded from her post at the shop window next to the inn. "Where is Miss Jones?" she asked. Her eyes skimmed over Augusta, over Grace, and Lady Dewitt. "What have you done with her?" she demanded of Whewett. Her eyes skewed back to Grace. She had seen that blue serge suit before, and those bold brown eyes. Her face clenched into a fist of suspicion. "You're Miss Jones!" she proclaimed loudly in an accusing voice.

"I?" Grace asked, assuming an astonished face and employing her mature voice.

"This is Miss Farnsworth," Augusta volunteered.

"May I know who *you* are?" Grace asked haughtily, "and what interest any of us are to you?"

"You know who I am right enough. Don't go with him, missie. He's a depraved lunatic and not a lord at all, as he's trying to con you, he is." Her eyes slid to the lozenge on his carriage door, causing a pang of alarm.

Grace looked to Whewett, her lips trembling. "What *have* you been up to, Whewett, to give this good woman such a low opinion of you?"

"He's deceiving you!" Mrs. Sempleton insisted. "I'll call the constable. Don't get into his rig, or you'll never get out alive."

"Yes, pray call the constable," Whewett said politely. "I want to have you arrested for being a common scold. Dunking, like a witch, is the traditional punishment. Good day, Mrs. Sempleton. Hop in, Grace," he said, turning to his companion.

Grace was not tardy to escape into the carriage, with Gussie and Whewett right after her. The door was closed, and with Mrs. Sempleton still looking on in disgusted rapture, they were off.

"I knew it," Grace said. "We should have given the poor soul some explanation." She noticed Augusta's curious look and fell silent.

"It was inevitable," Whewett agreed. He looked out the window and waved at the woman. She was so distraught, she waved back before she thought what she was about. In lieu of going to the constable, she took the story to her husband. He was so well accustomed to her imaginings that he paid very little heed.

"Who was that woman, Papa?" Augusta asked.

"Just the village lunatic. She is mistaking Miss Farnsworth with her young sister. Pay her no heed," he answered, then was struck with the happy idea of diverting Gussie with the doll.

"Grandma had a skipping rope for you, too," Grace told her, "but we carelessly left it behind."

"Good," Augusta said with great feeling.

The journey passed happily with chatter of Augusta's trip to Ireland, and a game of "bury all your horses." They stopped for a change of team and luncheon with Lady Dewitt at an inn in Maidstone and again just past Ashford for fresh horses and dinner. It was a long day's drive. Darkness had fallen on the last lap from Ashford to Dover. Augusta rested her head on her father's shoulder and fell into a doze. Grace, too, was tired, but found sleep impossible in a jostling carriage.

"Whewett, are you asleep?" she asked softly.

"No, I thought you were. It isn't much farther. There—Gussie is snoring. She's tuckered out."

"Was it a horrid thing we did, keeping Lady Healy from knowing her granddaughter?"

"I feel some slight regret, but they would not have hit it off. Grandma has a young relative to think and dream of in her declining days. The fortune was always meant for Gussie, so there is no crime or sin in it. Are you having qualms of conscience?"

"Yes. I miss the old harpy, too."

"So do I," he answered, but in a dreamy way that suggested his mind was elsewhere. They sank into silence.

211

It was late when they arrived. Grace saw no more of Downsfield than a long facade of pale stone and an impressive carved oak doorway. A few windows in the lower story showed light. "We're home," Whewett said with a certain proud satisfaction.

Augusta was awakened to enter the house, rubbing her eyes sleepily. Grace looked at a vast expanse of marble hallway, with a view of an elegant saloon off to the right and a graceful staircase curving upward. Before she had time to examine anything in detail, there was a flurry of running servants, of lighting more lamps, of ordering food, and arranging rooms for Miss Farnsworth and for Lady Dewitt, whose carriage was following not far behind them.

"The blue suite for Miss Farnsworth," Whewett said, and a maid took her upstairs.

Grace looked around the well-appointed chamber, with blue velvet window hangings and a pale ivory carpet spangled with gold roses and greenery. Mahogany furnishings reflected the gold of lamplight in their cherry depths. An adjoining door gave her a glimpse of a private drawing room. This was obviously one of the better guest rooms, not the sort of accommodation a governess would expect. A canopied bed in the corner invited her to recline, but she must freshen herself to go below and meet Lady Dewitt when she arrived. They were all to have a late supper.

As she brushed out her curls, she was aware of her pale cheeks and drooping eyelids. She was hungry and felt that bread and meat might revive her to a more pleasing appearance. A light tap sounded at the door. Was she being called downstairs already? Lady Dewitt had not been that close behind them.

"Are you decent?" Whewett's voice called.

"More or less. Come in," she answered, before remembering the new proprieties that must now be exercised between them. The door opened, and Whowctt stepped in.

After a shave and a change of shirt, Whewett looked as fresh as a new penny. "Actually I am indocently frazzled," Grace said, unhappy with the contrast between them. "I look like an unmade bed, with my skirts all rumpled."

Whewett displayed a very proper disinterest in all her dishevelment. "You look good to me," he said with a glowing eye. "Is your room satisfactory? Have you got everything you need—hot water, towels?"

"I am wallowing in the very lap of luxury. I will be spoiled with all this pampering."

He handed her a check. "Here is your payment, to begin the process."

"Thank you," she said and accepted it without demur. "Is your sister here yet?"

"No, I wanted to speak to you before she arrives. We should go downstairs, I expect, but between us two disreputable thespians, one more rendezvous in your bedchamber can hardly matter."

"What is it you want to discuss?" She saw the air of uncertainty that had settled over Whewett and felt he was about to suggest some further payment for her chore.

"I made a very stupid, awkward proposal to you before, Grace," he said. Her pulse raced, and her breathing accelerated to light, shallow breaths. "I have been rehearsing it these few days in order to perform better this time. I am not looking for a mother to Augusta, and not for a marriage of convenience, either. Your reputation will recover from our escapade, for no one knows of it but Mrs. Townsend, and I don't believe she knows any of your friends. You would be well treated and happy with Mary in Ireland."

Her pulse slowed, and a droop of disappointment settled on her shoulders. This did not sound like the hoped-for proposal, but a rationalization for withdrawing his offer. Yet he wore the tense air of a man on the edge of a momentous speech. "Yes," she agreed in confusion.

"All this is by way of making clear what I am about. What you behold before you is a foolish romantic, trying to tell you he loves you. Please don't mention age. You are not one second too young for me. Am I too old—"

"No!" she exclaimed swiftly. "Don't be foolish, Whewett." She looked, and through the eyes of love, she beheld a handsome, dashing young gentleman. "Oh, but you can't marry me. I am a governess, and not a very good one, either."

"You are the most delightful, enchanting, madcap governess I have ever met, and you will make a superb Lady Whewett."

She looked at him hopefully, with wonder in her heart that he could love her. "Do you think Augusta will like me, though?"

He grasped her hands. "*I* love you, Grace. I love you to distraction, and if you love me, that is all that really matters, for I cannot conceive of your being a wicked stepmother to Augusta. Gussie has opened her heart to modistes and clerks' daughters. She will love you."

"We haven't really known each other very long," she said doubtfully. "You and I, I mean." His fingers tightened convulsively on hers, and his expression warmed.

"Not long, but well, and under peculiarly intimate circumstances. What other couple was ever pitched together as we were? Why, I have seen you grow from an awkward adolescent to a ravishing young lady, right before my very eyes—in about two minutes, in my carriage."

She was reassured by the compliment but said, "I am not ravishing, Whewett."

"I think you are. You ravish me. In pinafores and in pigtails, in shiny suit and dashing bonnet, for better or worse, in sprained ankle and in health." His voice assumed a husky burr as he spoke.

His arms closed around her, crushing her against him for a long, heart pounding moment. "Are you sure?" she asked.

He tipped her head back from his shoulder and gazed at her, his eyes glowing, while a smile hovered on his lips. "I was never so certain of anything in my life. Right in there with death and taxes," he said, before he lowered his head to kiss her.

Even on tiptoe, she had to stretch to get her arms around his neck. In frustration, he lifted her up from the ground, with his hands around her waist, and his lips clinging hungrily to hers.

"You can put me down now," she said, after a long kiss. Sense returned when her feet were again on the floor. "Oh! What about Mary? I am supposed to be working for her," she remembered.

"No, for me, you lazy little squab. Now get to work."

She resumed the first duties of a new fiancée, and her performance caused no doubt that she would provide an even more satisfactory wife than she had a daughter.